THE KILLER

Patrícia Melo

Translated
by Clifford E. Landers

BLOOMSBURY

First published in 1995 by Companhia das Letras, Brazil as *O Matador*

This edition published 1998

Copyright © Patrícia Melo 1995
Translation © Clifford E. Landers 1997

The moral right of the author and translator have been asserted

Bloomsbury Publishing Plc, 38 Soho Square, London W1V 5DF

A CIP catalogue record for this book
is available from the British Library

ISBN 07475 3524 8

10 9 8 7 6 5 4 3 2

Typeset by Hewer Text Composition Services, Edinburgh
Printed in Great Britain by Clays Ltd, St Ives Plc

THE KILLER

PART ONE

I

It all began when I lost a wager.

I sat down in the chair. Arlete, the owner of the salon, placed a sheet over my shirt. My eyes on the ads, the pretty women plastered on the wall. A discreet shade; no one would notice. Arlete didn't understand a thing when I said I wanted to dye my hair chestnut-blond. She laughed, thinking I was kidding. That was the wager. São Paulo had lost, two to nothing, to Palmeiras.

Arlete put a sticky paste in my hair and said the stuff had to stay there for twenty minutes. The plastic cap made everything worse. I felt ridiculous. I think men who do that are ridiculous. I had brought a razor; the wager included the mustache. I looked at the mirror, timidly. I'd had a mustache for five years, ever since I saw a Charles Bronson film on television. I recalled that my life without a mustache had been shit. My guardian angels, God, my protectors, were all there in my mustache. Seeing my indecision, Arlete took the razor from my hands and started shaving me. She was tanned, a beautiful body, firm legs. Her breasts brushed against my

3

arm and face, she breathed close to my mouth, diabolically. I remembered when we used to fuck on the couch at her place, after her paralyzed father went to sleep. I got the urge. Arlete drew back, like she didn't understand, but I grabbed her body, pressed our mouths together. We kissed. I leaned my weight against the chair, and we fell, locked together. I kneeled, we kneeled, I lifted her yellow dress and felt that powerful thing all around us. Arlete, the mare, her bikini marks, her wet pussy; me, the rider, my troop of horses, my shaft discharging a great liquid tree with a leafy crown, full of flowers. I had the impression that it all happened in a short time, five seconds, something really fast, but then Arlete opened her eyes, started waving her arms around and screaming like a magpie. She grabbed me by the arm, stuck my head in the sink, rinsed my hair, cursing, moaning, bellowing like some crazy person in an asylum. We went to the combing area, Arlete demanding that I keep my back to the mirror. When I finally got permission to look at the result, I was surprised: my hair was completely blond. Real blond, like those English rock singers.

I always thought of myself as an ugly man. There's lots of curves in my face, lots of flesh too; I never liked it. My toad-like eyes, my rounded nose; I always avoided mirrors. That day it was different. I stood there, admiring the image of that human being who wasn't me; a blond, someone unfamiliar, a stranger. It wasn't only the hair that had become lighter. My skin, my eyes, everything had a glow to it, a frame of light. Suddenly, all my features had become harmonious. The mouth, which had always had a downward turn to it, still turned down, the nose was still rounded, the eyelids were still puffy, but all that was nothing because there was something bigger, more important: the frame. There was

4

light in my face, and it wasn't the artificial light of reflectors. It was that light you see in religious images, the light of someone illuminated by God. That's how I felt, close to God.

Arlete was in agony at my silence. I couldn't take my eyes away from the mirror.

It's good, I said. I like it.

You actually like that piece of shit?

It's not a piece of shit.

Yes, it is, a piece of shit. You look awful. You're not leaving here looking like that.

I wasn't lying, and it was obvious that I was going to leave there looking like that. The dye colored something very deep inside me. It colored my self-confidence, my self-esteem. It was the first time, in twenty-two years, that I had looked in the mirror and not felt like putting my fist through it. I kissed Arlete and left happy, thinking that I'd spent most of my life wanting to be some other guy.

Mappin,
No time to waste,
Mappin,
The time is right,
Mappin,
It's all on sale!

When I was a boy, I loved listening to the Mappin jingle. Gradiente VCR, four heads, remote control. The Gradiente one-year warranty. Self-cleaning heads. Comes with stand. One-sixty cash or two payments of eighty. Families, toys, installments, credit plans. Take advantage of it! I love going to Mappin. Final days of the sale. Bed-linen sets. Sales. Everything for your car, don't miss it. Sales. Mappin.

I looked around for a pretty salesgirl. All of them were pretty in that uniform that looks like a stewardess's. I picked a brunette.

I bet you have good taste.

She smiled. She had a tooth with a broken tip. Charming.

How do you like your husband to dress?

I'm not married, she said. Green light.

But you have a boyfriend. I was looking at undershorts.

No. She was very young, a ripe peach.

So tell me, if I was your boyfriend – she laughed, I pretended not to notice – if I was your boyfriend, how would you like me to dress?

Are you a salesman?

I worked at a used-car lot. I would get fired soon, when they found out I'd been driving around every night, in a different car each time.

Yes.

Then you should wear a dress-shirt.

Her name was Cledir and she'd been working at Mappin for two months. She was studying typing, she had a sick mother, her father had died in a car accident. I found all that out while coming and going in the fitting room, with Cledir at my heels suggesting necessary changes.

We picked two light-colored shirts, which go with everything, two T-shirts, a black belt and a pair of Levi's. Cledir laughed when I said Levi's; they weren't Levi's, they were jeans. I say Levi's because when I was little, denim pants were Levi's. Levi's were all there was, smuggled in from Argentina. I always wanted a pair, but I didn't have the money. I never had a pair of Levi's; I didn't say that to Cledir. She laughed a lot at the story, and I thought

6

that sometimes I have that power to make people laugh. It's good.

I picked up a tie just to fool around. Will you show me how to tie a knot? I asked. We were inside a fitting room. I wrapped my hands around her waist and could smell the scent of Arlete's pussy on my face. How could I have forgotten to wash? Could Cledir detect it?

It's easy. You just need to bring the two ends together, then even them up like this, bring the smaller part back, then run it through the front. Her eyes were sad: her father, the lack of a father. I felt sorry for her.

This is very complicated, I said. I think we should go somewhere and you can explain it to me better. I tried to kiss her. The smell, the enzymes, the bacteria of Arlete's pussy were driving me crazy. My sex, a wild stallion tied down.

You want me to lose my job?

Do you like barbecue?

I opened a charge account, wrote a bad check (the next day I'd ask for an advance at the place where I worked) and left, dying for the time to go by quickly.

At ten o'clock Cledir, wearing a white dress with ruffles on the hip, left Mappin and got into my gunmetal-blue car.

I wanted to take her to a motel and fuck all night, but I had agreed to stop by Gonzaga's bar and show my cousin Robinson the pay-off of the wager. Actually, I could do that some other time, some other day, but the truth is I wanted to go there; I was looking good with that hair, the dress-shirt, the jeans and the car that wasn't mine but went with the package. Besides which, I was in the company of Cledir, a knockout of a brunette who, I had decided, was going to be my girlfriend. I might even marry her. I said, Cledir, I have to stop by Gonzaga's and then I'm going to take you for a

7

night you'll never forget. Maybe Robinson would lend me enough to pay for the barbecue and the motel.

I parked, got out, opened the door for the smashing brunette, and went in. I went into Gonzaga's with my girlfriend. Marcão, Galego, Suel, everybody drinking beer, except Robinson, who hadn't arrived yet. Everybody stopped talking. They stared at us, all of them, me blond in a dress-shirt, with that marvelous brunette; they couldn't stop staring.

What's with you guys? I asked.

Nobody answered. All of them had their mouths open, including Gonzaga, the owner of the bar. Three guys playing pool. They stopped and stared at us.

This is Cledir, my girlfriend.

Nothing. Nobody said a thing.

I pulled out a chair for Cledir, who was starting to look self-conscious. That was when Suel started laughing. He looked at me and laughed. I was never a buddy of Suel's; now and then he'd ask me to buy him a beer, I would, and that was it. Everybody in the neighborhood knew about his reputation. I never had any desire to find out; he could go fuck himself was my philosophy.

What's with you? What's so funny? I asked.

Jeez, you really went blond, he said. You look funny.

You think it's funny, Suel?

Shit yes it's funny. You look like a gringo.

So you think I'm a faggot.

Shit, man, you show up here lookin' like a gringo, shit yes I think it's funny. What's the fuckin' problem?

The problem is you called me a faggot.

He laughed. Like hell I did.

There's a type of laugh that makes me crazy. I couldn't let him get away with that.

8

Tomorrow. Six o'clock in front of Tonho's bar. We're going to have a duel.

Suel turned white.

What kinda bullshit is this, man?

I pulled Cledir by the arm and headed out.

You understood perfectly, I said.

I took Cledir home, went by the lot to return the car, then went to sleep. I'd lost the desire to fuck that night.

The next day, I woke with a toothache and didn't go to work. I was sorry I'd suggested the duel; it was a dumb thing to do, a real piece of stupidity. I was trying to act the tough guy to impress Cledir and I shafted myself. Suel was one badass black dude. They said in the neighborhood that his profession was stealing tape players. He could have rough friends, and for sure he'd know his way around guns. I was afraid. I'd never held a gun. Suel would win; I'd have to apologize to him. I don't mind apologizing. All the time I'm screwing up and apologizing for it. Another possibility was not to show up at Tonho's. Result: Suel might get really mad and catch me on the street, unprepared. It was better to try to negotiate. I took half a bottle of painkillers and went looking for him. His mother, his buddies, his brother; nobody knew where he was. I left messages everywhere. At five o'clock my tooth was throbbing with pain and I still hadn't found the guy. I went to my uncle's place, fetched a .28-caliber rifle, put it in an empty fluorescent light-bulb box that was there; it fit perfectly. I went to Tonho's. This was the plan: I'd try to talk with him, do the I drank too much and let's forget it bit, but if I needed it, the gun was there, close by. You never know what's going to happen.

On the bus, on the way to Tonho's bar, I nearly vomited

on the passenger sitting in front of me. Damned painkillers. I was wondering if there wasn't some way of solving the problem without going there. There wasn't. I got off the bus, my tooth giving me hell, and walked the two blocks to Tonho's. Right away, things started going wrong. Cledir was sitting at the counter, and when she saw me she ran toward me, tears in her voice, begging me not to go any further with that foolishness. And I'd been thinking about not seeing Cledir again. A good opportunity, I thought. Cledir was sobbing, begging, don't do it, don't ruin your life. It's OK, Cledir. No need to cry, you're right. Two-bedroom apartment, no security deposit, don't let the chance pass by. I'm not going to fight him. Furnished kitchen. I'm going to marry you. Everything you need for your very own home. I'm going to knuckle down at the used-car lot, change my life for the better. Move up to the best. Good things ran through my head, but I didn't mention them to Cledir. What I said was: No fuckin' way. Really, there's no accounting for how a guy can do a stupid thing like that. There's just one explanation: fate. Before we're born, somebody, I don't know who, God maybe, God defines exactly how he's going to fuck with our lives. That's it. That was my theory. God only thinks about people when he has to decide how he's going to destroy them. When he's pressed for time, he comes up with a war or a hurricane and kills them in droves, without having to give any thought at all. With me, he gave it some thought.

That guy's going to learn not to go around calling other people faggots, I said.

He didn't call you a faggot, he called you a gringo.

Same thing. Faggot and gringo are the same thing.

I don't know where I got that from either. I went outside, carrying my rifle in its box. Suel showed up right away. He was unarmed, holding hands with his girlfriend. That gave me a lot of courage. I took out the rifle. Kneeled in the firing position. Go for your gun, Suel. He said I must be kidding. We're friends, he said. Like shit we were friends, but I could perfectly well have followed his cue and put an end to the matter.

Go for your gun, I insisted.

He laughed, not knowing whether to believe it. Suel wanted to drop it, and that gave me courage. I looked at the people standing in the doorway of Tonho's bar, all of them observing me, and that gave me courage. I took aim.

If you plan to kill me, Máiquel, you'll have to shoot me in the back, he said.

Suel turned his back on me and went jiveassing away, holding hands with his girl.

Go ahead and shoot, he said, kill me from behind.

I shot the first round. Suel hit the ground; he must have died instantly. His girlfriend screamed and tried to drag him to the car. I shot again without taking aim and caught Suel in the head. That's how it was, just the way it went down. He was the first person I ever killed. Till that happened, I was just a guy who sold used cars and rooted for the São Paulo Soccer Club.

2

Jokes about blacks, about the Portuguese, about the Japanese. I hate jokes. I don't like it when they're told to me. I don't laugh, I don't think they're funny. But with the joke about the jack, which was told to me by an Italian uncle when I was five, the opposite happened. I've become fixated on it.

A dirt road, deserted. A guy traveling by himself gets out of the car for the simple operation of changing a flat tire and realizes he doesn't have a jack. A dot of light at the top of a mountain gives him hope: where there's a man, there's a jack. The guy walks toward the light. The hermit must have a jack. Will he lend it to him? Sure. The jack might be broken. It's not broken. Somebody may have stolen it. Nobody stole it, but the hermit simply won't lend it to him. Of course he won't lend it, the hermit's a faggot. There's no way he'll lend it. That idiot isn't about to let anybody borrow his jack. Absolutely not. As far as that imbecile is concerned, the rest of the world can fuck itself. Evil thoughts form in the solitary man's head, while his liver is macerated by the enzymes of hate. He doesn't even realize he's walked five miles. He stops in front of the shack. Knocks on the door. An elderly man opens it, smiles gently, says can I help you? Shove your goddamn jack up your ass.

I've often dreamed about that joke. I invented a face for the hermit and put my own face on the solitary traveler. I am the solitary traveler with a flat tire. My entire life works that way: a flat tire and somebody who refuses to lend me a jack. I expect the worst from life, the worst from fate, from people, from nature, from whatever. When I think about doing something I give up because I know it won't work out. And if I do begin, I only go halfway. I leave everything half done.

People kill and then run away. Or they're caught and pardoned. They're released on insufficient evidence. They're found guilty and run away. With me it wouldn't be like that.

You have soft skin, says a man with the face of an Indian. Two others hold me down and the Indian tries to screw me, while I scream for the guards to get me out of this cell.

Cledir telling me to run. I couldn't move my feet. Suel there on the ground, his girlfriend kissing the dead body, crying, Tonho at the door to the bar, the cars, the buses, all of them slowing down to get a look at the scene of the crime. The headline in the paper at the news-stand: Armored car heist gang captured. Run, Cledir said. Call the police. I'm going to turn myself in. Get away from here, get out of the city. I think it was Cledir who put me in a taxi.

The street was full of people. People returning from work; they hadn't killed anybody. Their wives and children waiting, dinner, TV, the nest. Free of guilt. Free of toothache. And I had just killed a man. I had just killed a man and I was devastated. And had a toothache. And I had skipped work.

I couldn't get the image of the girl kissing the corpse out of my mind. Why did I kill Suel? I wanted to know, wanted someone to explain why I killed Suel. I went to Robinson's house, totally wiped out. I wanted to be arrested, tried and sentenced. I hoped Suel had a brother to kill me right there, while Robinson paid off the taxi and took me inside. I was trembling, my tooth hurt. Robinson sat me down on the sofa and made me a strong cup of coffee.

In my family, men don't usually cry. Not because of machismo, although we are macho. We don't cry because we don't laugh either, we don't hug, we don't kiss, and we don't use kind words. We don't show anything that's going on inside our skin. That's how we're raised. My grandfather was like that, my father was like that, and my children will be brought up the same way. I never cried in front of anyone, except that day. I cried, I sobbed: I killed a man. Call the police, I'm going to turn myself in.

Robinson said, no, you're not going to turn yourself in. He gave me some money, the key to his car, and told me to go to São José dos Campos. Leave the car in the parking lot across from the bus station and take a bus to Goiânia. In Goiânia take another bus to any small town with a hotel where you can lay low for a month.

I started the car, went half a block, and the engine stalled. Robinson, who was still on his porch watching me leave, came running; we tried to get the car started by pushing, didn't succeed. Marcão, the mechanic, towed the car and we went to his shop. It'll just take five minutes, Marcão said. Robinson had some cocaine; it was the first time in my life that I'd snorted. I don't go for drugs, I just wanted to see what it was like. They stayed there fixing the car, and I went to the john. The coke wasn't having any effect; my face was still the same.

I thought: I'll stand in front of the mirror for fifteen minutes to see if anything happens. I wanted to see the cocaine in action, but nothing happened in the fifteen minutes. I'll do a hundred deep knee bends. I did, and nothing. Five hundred deep knee bends. I did five hundred deep knee bends, and still nothing; cocaine isn't for me. I'll stand on my head for fifteen minutes. I stood on my head for fifteen minutes; the coke still wasn't working. I went back to the office; they were still trying to fix the car. I did two more lines. I was tense, so I went to get some air. I wanted to see if the cocaine would kick in. I'll run around the block sixteen times. I did sixteen laps, and nothing, I didn't feel a thing. I'll hop down to the church on one leg. I went; nothing happened. I'll run back on tiptoe. I came back; nothing happened, absolutely nothing. The car was ready, and Robinson bawled me out: Why were you gone so long?

I wasn't gone for long.

You were gone two hours. What's with you? You want to go to jail?

We said goodbye. I was feeling better. I still remembered the girl kissing the corpse, but something told me that was natural, that sometimes in life we have to do that, kiss corpses.

It was four am and I was leaving São Paulo. I'd stay away for a month, two months, however long it took for things to cool down. There was an awful taste in my mouth, the taste of medicine, the crap they use to cut cocaine. I thought of stopping by Gonzaga's for some coffee. From there I'd hit the highway.

As soon as he saw me, Gonzaga held out his wet hand, that damp and practical hand gripping my hand, smiling and saying that I could have anything I wanted, on the house. From now on that's how it would be, for good, I deserved it, I was brave, he said, and now that's how it'll be, everything you want. He was happy because I'd killed Suel. Suel is a miserable son of a bitch. He stole the tape player from my sister's car. Everybody hates Suel. I hate Suel, he said. I was surprised; all I wanted was a cup of coffee. I'd planned to pay for the coffee. From now on, starting now, your money's no good here.

A vehicle pulled up in front of the bar and only then did the cocaine start to take effect. I felt my body transformed into an iceberg. A trap, I thought, the cop was coming toward me. It really was a cop, uniform, boots, police regulation pistol, and Gonzaga said in a loud voice, looking right at the cop, it was him. It was him who killed Suel. I went blind for an instant. Gonzaga is a son of a bitch, a total idiot, and my legs wouldn't respond, and before these phrases could form in my head, before I could think that Gonzaga was an idiot, the cop was slapping me on the back and saying that he admired brave men. He said this and something snapped inside me. Iceberg. The cop got some meat pies and cans of Coke and stamped out, boots, weapon, uniform, getting into the vehicle, where five other cops were waiting, all of them waving at me, not actually waving their hands but waving with their eyes, something men traditionally do as a greeting when they're unacquainted but admire each other.

I also had meat pies and a Coca-Cola, all free. I got in the car and said to myself: I'm strong. I'm good. I'm innocent. There's no reason to run away.

3

Noon. I wanted to go on sleeping, sleeping for several days, but somebody was knocking insistently on the kitchen door. The toothache; I didn't remember feeling any pain the night before. Why hadn't I run away? I was real brave in Gonzaga's bar, I felt strong, my teeth didn't ache. Maybe it was the painkillers; I was still taking a lot of painkillers. Or the cocaine. It wasn't the coke; coke just made me feel scared, real scared, the same kind of scared I feel now, a chill running through my veins. The knocking at the door got louder. Police, you're under arrest. Why hadn't I run away last night? I fooled myself into thinking I was safe just because a cop said: So you killed Suel, who cares? Who cares about some black guy? Who cares about you? Nobody cares. Nobody cares about anybody. A man is just a piece of meat, all right? Pork, beef, who cares? It might be a bluff. That son of a bitch would be sure to testify at my trial; he'd say that I admitted the crime in Gonzaga's bar. Robinson would kill me when he found out I'd given up on running away. By this time I could be on the way to Goiânia, free, in a clean bed in some cheap hotel, with decent food. Why had I stayed?

I took the rifle to the bathroom. If it was the police I'd say OK, I killed Suel. You can take me, just let me go to the bathroom first. I had bullets, I'd put one in my brain. They could hang me too. My life was shit; that damned toothache, it wouldn't be so bad to die that day.

The door, the knocking, the tooth throbbing, I went to open it. It was a skinny kid, holding a pig. What is it? Mr Baldani told me to bring you this. I didn't know who Baldani was and I was embarrassed to ask. And he told me to say congratulations, he said, the skinny kid. Congratulations to you. The kid handed me the pig and left.

I got a pig as a present. A soft, pink pig I can eat with potatoes and rice. Or with broccoli. I love broccoli. The pig had sad little eyes, just like Cledir's. I decided I wouldn't kill it; my tooth was aching a lot and I wouldn't be able to chew anything. I thought it was strange to get a pig as a present.

I spent the day at home, not eating, just taking painkillers. The pig played with my sneaker. I slept, woke up, took painkillers, dreamed, the Beatles singing. I have a neighbor who loves the Beatles. I dreamed I was driving at seventy-five miles an hour, John Lennon beside me, with a guitar; I didn't know he was John Lennon. Where've you been? I said. In a queue, he answered. You see how people's heads work. I never paid any attention to the Beatles; I don't like rock. My neighbor doesn't change the record.

Why did they give me a pig? Could this Baldani guy be a cop? What if he's a relative of Suel's? Somebody calling me a pig, no, not that. I took a shower, shaved, blood pressure dropped. I had to lean against the wall to keep from falling. It was stupid not to run away the night before. Why hadn't the police arrested me? Isn't it the police's job to catch murderers? I was a murderer, a son of a bitch. I killed a man for no reason, left that girl all alone, crying over her boyfriend's body.

My heart was like a bees' nest, nothing but bees. I couldn't take staying in the house any longer. When I opened the door I found a pile of packages on the threshold: cigarettes, ground beef, rum and flowers. There was also a note, in a child's handwriting: Thank you, Máiquel. Another: Serves Suel right, in a woman's handwriting. Criminals must die, a man's handwriting. He died because he was of no use to society, typewritten. The pig, of course. I was given the pig as a present for killing Suel. And cigarettes. Meat. Rum and beer. People were pleased. I liked the gifts.

I left the house warily. I still didn't understand everything. Almost everything. I was beginning to understand. The neighbors smiled. Children, mothers, maids, prostitutes, news vendors, citizens. They all smiled at me. At the bakery, a lady kissed me on the cheek and said: You can count on me, rollers in her hair, a decent woman like my mother. You can count on me.

At Gonzaga's it was a party. Everybody shook my hand, asked me to tell them how I'd managed to kill Suel. I wasn't a liar, but I felt an urge. How did I kill Suel? Well, he bugged out his eyes and I shot. They exploded with laughter, I laughed too, even though the image of the girl kissing the body made me a bit sad. Can I eat anything I want, Gonzaga? Anything you want. I wasn't able to eat anything, because of the tooth. I asked for Coca-Cola.

Robinson came in, took me aside to the pool table. It's all they're talking about in the neighborhood, everybody's proud of you, he said. The police were really after Suel. He was about to be arrested, the son of a bitch. He was a mugger. He was a rapist, did you know that Suel raped a little girl? The detective at the 15th precinct is a friend of Marcão's, he told Marcão to tell you hello. I swear to God, man. Robinson talked nonstop; I needed another painkiller. I asked if he knew about the girl, Suel's girlfriend. Fuck her, he said. Yeah, that's right, I thought, fuck her.

I went home, took more painkillers, lay down. In the evening, Robinson brought some buddies of ours and we drank beer. I was sad. I don't know why. Everything was all right, but I was sad as shit. I lay down on the sofa, listening to the conversation. Soccer. It was cold and the pig went to sleep at my feet. I went to sleep too, with a toothache, listening to my pals howling with laughter.

After I killed Suel, a lot changed in my life. Logic stopped working. I was close to the edge, in the dark, going the wrong way down a one-way street, and yet everything was all right. Edges and the wrong way. I did everything wrong, nobody saw, and if they saw they paid no attention and if they paid any attention they forgot about it, because that's how life is. It's been said that everything ends up like that, in the sewer of oblivion.

The police didn't come for me the following day or any other day. When they saw me, they smiled. How's it going, man? Fine, I answered. Yeah, we arrested a dealer. We arrested a prostitute. We arrested some kids who were hanging out giving people a hard time. And they would leave. I received more gifts. People who used not to say hello started greeting me. Hello, Máiquel. Good evening, Máiquel. How are you? Fine, I'm fine, except for this toothache that's killing me.

I didn't go out of the house much. I stayed in, taking painkillers, trying to understand the other side of life. I still thought that the crime would have consequences, thought it was too soon to feel safe. A week later, I thought that everything was all right, there wasn't any danger anymore. I decided to return to work. Maybe I could come up with a good lie for Mr Paulo, my boss. Maybe he wouldn't fire me.

Everything was the same as usual at Novocar; lots of new cars in the storage area, a supercool gunmetal-brown Opala. There was also a yellow Maverick; it had been a long time since a Maverick came in. It's a sports car, I thought about taking Cledir for a ride in it, but Cledir wasn't my girlfriend anymore. The boss hasn't come in yet, said Janete, Mr Paulo's secretary. I had a tooth pulled. You did? Yes. She couldn't care less. A rich woman came in wanting to buy a motorcycle for her lover, a kid ten years younger than her. The give-me-your-youth, take-my-money kind of couple. Janete looked at me with the expression of somebody who doesn't have a toothache. Aren't you going to help her? Yes. The buyer was pretty, her hair smelled of flowers, her nails were red. Women like that know how to take care of themselves. And they also know how to make me look a fool. People like that woman make me feel ashamed of my shoes; her boyfriend had on a nice-looking pair of shoes, with a little gold chain, and me with those shitty navy-blue shoes. I'd like another salesman, she said, you're very ill-tempered. Wait here, I'll call another salesman. I wasn't ill-tempered. I had a toothache. I left and never went back to the dealership. He was going to fire me anyway. I thought about going back and telling him: Mr Paulo, I came here to say two things. The first is that I quit. And the second is that used-car dealers can go fuck themselves. But why bother? He wouldn't even let me speak; he'd speak first: You're fired. The only way would be if I went in without even saying hello, right off the bat vomiting out what I had to vomit: I quit. He could speak at the same time as me, louder: You're fired. Anyway, why was I suffering so much? I never liked working there: How much does it cost, how does the motor work, it's too expensive, can I take it for a test drive, what's that there? To tell the truth, every time I go into a dealership, my blood pressure drops. To this day, I feel a lack of energy, the desire to remain quietly in my corner. I never had the knack for those technical things: locksmiths, construction materials stores, lighting shops, all those places sap my energy.

Janitor wanted. Seeking doorman. Experienced accountant. Accountant's office seeks clerk. God forbid. Are you young and want to make money? Yes. Do you want to own your own business? Soap. I know what it's like, they recruit you to sell soap. You go there, take a two-day course, they catechize you, make you buy a ton of soap and you open your own business. You get all worked up and when you come back to reality you're unemployed and have a house full of soap. It happened to me; I read the ad in the paper and took the course along with a bunch of other suckers. I even bought the soap. Professional Services. Nice and tight. Demi-virgin needs experience. From ten pm to six am. Needs experience, that's a good one. Exotic girls; they think it sounds better in English. Pleasant companions for discreet people of discerning taste. Those whores are too fucking much. Look at this one: raging bull. Erotic video with animals. Student. I want to show what I've learned. She probably blows like a champ.

Now and then I looked for work, talked with some bore; he'd say he had to think it over, I wouldn't even go back. My tooth was still hurting. Sometimes I'd see animals on the walls; that's what too much painkiller does to you.

Pigs, like dogs, know how to love those who take good

care of them. I came to feel a certain affection for Gorby, my pig, though at night, when I got hungry, the thought crossed my mind to roast him with potatoes. Pork rind is really good. But I cared about him; he was a special pig, intelligent as hell.

One day I came home and found my white sneakers all chewed up. I was furious. You no-good pig, and here I am feeding him every day, letting him sleep in the house. I got a knife from the kitchen. I'm going to kill that pig. It was hard to grab him, but I grabbed him, stuck him between my legs, and was going to cut his head off, but I heard Cledir's voice calling me from the gate. Sweet Cledir. We hadn't seen each other since the day of the duel. I had even been thinking of looking for her. I took Gorby to the backyard. I opened the door for Cledir. She looked supergreat, in a blue skirt and white blouse. Hi, everything OK? She came in the way people do when they enter a place for the first time, taking in everything. Right off, she saw the damage.

What happened to the sneakers?

He ruined them.

The dog?

No. It was Gorby.

Who's Gorby?

Never mind that, Cledir. Have a seat.

Is it a cat?

Sit here.

Tell me. Why don't you want to tell me?

It's a pig.

You have a pig?

Yes.

How cute! Where is he?

He's in the yard.

Can I see him?

Why do you want to see him?

I just do, what's wrong with that?

This bothered me, showing the pig, having a pig in the house, how humiliating. Things start changing, you let them go on and on, and the first thing you know, you've got a pig living in your house. I never wanted a pig. People don't usually have pigs in their home. People don't like pigs. We eat pigs, that's normal. Cledir looked at Gorby with an affectionate expression, as if he was my son, a member of the family. That put me in a really shitty mood.

He's really quite clean, she said.

I'm going to kill him.

You're going to kill that pig?

Of course I am. What do you think I've got a pig in the house for?

We stopped talking, sat down, and that was when I realized the pig had eaten a piece of the sofa too. Son of a bitch.

I thought you were going to look me up, Cledir said.

I wasn't capable of doing anything, my heart, the bees. She stood up, opened her blouse. I could see her lovely breasts. She took off her skirt, a beautiful body, no tan lines, white as could be, lovely. She sat beside me. I didn't do anything. She kissed my face. I still didn't do anything.

Don't you want to? she asked.

No.

Why not?

I can't today. Some other time.

I had a toothache, that was why. Cledir started crying and it was only then that I felt desire for her. She was crying and trying to put on her clothes, didn't want me to touch her. I tried to explain. You don't understand, Cledir. I like you.

Let me go. I'm leaving. The desire came from some dark place, a place I don't know and can't control. My desire came from there and exploded, overcame the toothache and exploded. Don't leave. I'm leaving. Don't go. I pushed her to the floor. She tried to get up. I pulled her by the feet; she fell, hit her head, started to cry, and that made me feel more like entering the cavern, the abyss, the jungle. She crossed her legs, screamed; I covered her mouth with a cushion, opened her legs with my knee, stuck my cock into the jungle. It's like there's a wall inside her pussy; I broke through the wall and came.

I went to the bathroom, my prick was covered with blood. Holy shit, the wall, what a fuck-up. Cledir was a virgin. I ran back to the living room, but she'd already left.

My tooth was hurting so much that I felt like yanking it out with my bare hands. What a fuck-up. A virgin. I went to the mirror, opened my mouth wide and there the sucker was. My gum was real red, inflamed, and when I ran my tongue over it there was a bad taste, rotten. A big hole, big enough for the entire tip of my tongue. I stretched out and thought that dentists should invent a device that you put over your tooth and it absorbs all the pain. I took a large dose of painkillers. Poor Cledir, why did I do that? I broke out in a cold sweat, things went black, I fainted, and when I came to I made a decision. I wasn't going to suffer anymore because of the toothache. I would go to the dentist. Poor Cledir. It's going to cost a lot, it's going to hurt, they're going to fuck me, but fuck it, I thought. I couldn't take the pain any longer. Poor Cledir.

4

Dr Carvalho limped. He had taken a bullet in his leg when he lived in Rio de Janeiro. I pulled some guy's tooth and he didn't want to pay. Just think, I went to collect and got shot in the knee. Lucky I didn't die, he said. Violence is getting worse and worse. That was the end of Rio de Janeiro for me. I hate Rio de Janeiro. And São Paulo used to be better. The violence here, let's be honest about it, it's a jungle here. I moved to São Paulo thinking it would be better here. It's all the same; crime is running rampant.

I was ashamed to open my mouth, what with my shitty teeth. Dr Carvalho, in his white jacket, his white shoes, his hands smelling of soap, would be disgusted when he saw all that rottenness. Are you the one who killed Suel? The point-blank question startled me. I didn't answer; fortunately, the dental mirror was blocking my tongue. Dr Carvalho is a strange man, he has enormous hands. He told me he was in favor of the death penalty. There are crimes that only the death penalty can solve, he said, while he looked at my teeth with the mirror. Your teeth are in terrible shape. I'm in favor of the death penalty. I thumb my nose at anyone who thinks otherwise. This human-rights business is a joke. They're not human, the rapists, the kidnappers, they're not human. You should have seen the guy who shot me in the knee. His eyes. An animal. After I was shot in the leg, I became a Lombrosian. Do you know who Lombroso was? Lombroso formulated the theory of the born criminal. A genius, that Lombroso. The guy is born with it, the tendency toward crime, understand? There's talent for the piano. For painting, understand? The same with crime. It's difficult to get away from it. Impossible to correct, understand? Dr Carvalho tapped my front tooth with the handle of the mirror. How did you let this happen to your mouth? I felt ashamed in Dr Carvalho's presence. I felt awful. I remembered my pig. It's not in science that I seek my support, he said. God. It's God who gives me the answers. I studied Revelation, Acts, the Epistle to the Romans. I know what I'm talking about. The apostle Paul, for example, Chapter XXV, Verse 10: I stand at Caesar's judgment seat, where I ought to be judged. A very intelligent man, Dr Carvalho. It's just the back one that hurts, I said. The back one? The back one is rotten. You know what the apostle Paul meant by that? No, I don't know. He meant that judgment here on earth is just, it's acceptable. It's correct. It's not only God who can judge. Man can, man must judge. Does this tooth here hurt? No. It'll begin to hurt very, very soon. An impressive cavity. Never saw anything like it. Christ too. Christ acknowledged the possibility. Pilate, when he was interrogating Christ, irritated because Christ didn't answer his questions, said: Do you know your fate is in my hands? Christ's reply was: God gave you that power. In other words, Christ, Christ himself, acknowledged that not only God, but man also, at God's command, man could kill. Pilate had that power, Christ acknowledged it, and Christ was the Son of God, you know. All of your back teeth are affected. There's not a good one among them. Therefore, that business about thou shalt not kill only goes so far. St Thomas Aquinas himself says thou shalt kill if necessary, kill in the name of the law, Thomas Aquinas says. I mean, that's not exactly what he says, but it's almost that. I'm adapting, you understand? What he means is that whoever kills in the name of justice is not a criminal because it's not a crime, understand? The death penalty, in this case, is a right of society, it's not a crime. It's a right, not a crime, a right. Mind you, a God-given right. Do you brush your teeth regularly? I lied and said I did. I dislike brushing my teeth. Your brushing is very poor, that's why your gums bleed so much. My gums never stopped bleeding. Robbery with homicide, rape with homicide, and kidnapping with homicide; to me that should carry the death penalty. I read in the paper the other day that some people from the National Medical Council held a protest against the death penalty. It drove me crazy. The assholes said that a legal error is unacceptable. A medical error is fine with them. What about the poor devils they kill in hospitals? They say that it's the country's overall poverty that generates violence. Generates violence, generates pollution, generates disease, generates whatever, but it doesn't generate rapist sons of bitches. It doesn't generate that. Right?

Dr Carvalho took the mirror out of my mouth, looked at me like he was my own father. The tooth that's hurting you we can deal with. We can pull it. Treatment is expensive, you know. You need to take care of the other teeth too. If not, three years from now you won't have any teeth at all. You'll have to use dentures. How old are you? Twenty-two. A shame, so young.

My tooth was hurting like shit. What would you charge to pull this tooth?

I can do the treatment, he said.

I don't have any money.

You don't have to pay. I like you. I like what you did to Suel. The black son of a bitch deserved to die. I hate blacks. I'm a racist. Blacks are making our lives unbearable.

I didn't say anything. I dislike talking about Suel. Where could his girlfriend be? Dr Carvalho's eyes gleamed like stars. He hates blacks. Red light, who cares?

I'm going to tell you something, son. You have lousy teeth. I'm a dentist. I have a problem and you have lousy teeth. We can help one another. You help me, I'll help you. I'll fix your teeth for free and you'll do something for me. Agreed?

I want to have good teeth.

Killing a bastard, that's what I want from you.

I didn't say anything. A wave was forming in my sea. I locked my eyes on his. Dr Carvalho lowered his head. I have a fifteen-year-old daughter, a little flower. They ruined her. They raped my daughter as she was returning from school. You take care of your children, try to spare them suffering, and a guy like that comes along and ruins everything.

I remembered Cledir. Cledir's dry pussy chafed my cock.

I didn't report it to the police. You think I'd let those men examine her? No. My daughter was already humiliated once. Poor Cledir.

I didn't at all like the idea of having to kill another guy. But my tooth was hurting like hell.

5

I saw the sky was blue, saw naked women on the news-stand. Camila, fox of the year. Less than an hour since I'd left the dentist's office and that great feeling of being free from pain had already gone away. That's what man is: a forgetter. He forgets everything. He forgets the good things. The bad things he deposits at the bottom of the sea inside him. I have that sea. Those waves. Man is no good. The essence of man, the material he's made of, is something black and stinking. Our petroleum. Unconnected ideas. Sometimes I think such things.

A man to kill. That bothered me. His prick didn't want to go in; he spit in her pussy. Spit in her face too, while he came. Dr Carvalho gave me a photograph of him. Ezequiel. Suel, Suel's girlfriend, words embracing each other. The name of a prophet, an ordinary guy, with no expression at all. He didn't have the face of a fucker. I could hire somebody to kill Ezequiel. Maybe Marcão would lend me some money. I'd get a job and could repay him. It's good to feel you can control your life.

I stuck the photo in my pocket and walked toward the shop. Robinson was there. They had coke. We snorted, drank beer, I watched them stripping a car. The talk about nothing at all relaxed me. I felt everything was easier, all right; what was there left for me to do? What special thing was waiting for me? I can sell shoes, peel potatoes, anything. Fuck it. I can kill too. It's easy to kill: you pick up the revolver, pull the trigger, that's all. A simple gesture. Dying is what's hard. Everything OK, everything was OK, wasn't it? Marcão started singing a pretty song: You're something really fine, baby you're all mine, more than I ever dreamed of. I think it's by Tim Maia. Robinson started singing too: You're more than I dreamed of, more than I ever thought, I'm happy, I'm happy now. I started singing too and suddenly all three of us were around the car, singing and dancing and drinking, smoking, snorting and chopping a car. I thought it very pretty. It's like something out of a movie, I said. They were singing loudly and didn't hear. The carburetor refused to come out no matter what. Marcão stopped singing, became serious, strange. Robinson stopped singing too. I didn't want them to stop. Sing, you pieces of shit, you're everything to me, I continued, more than I ever dreamed of, let's sing, Robinson. They didn't want to sing, they wanted to take out the carburetor. Everything became so meaningless, so sad, a shop full of junk. I stopped singing too and felt sad. That's how life is: you're singing your favorite song and then all of a sudden you're not singing anymore. Let me pull out the carburetor, I said. I pulled hard, busted a hose, it was tough to get out. The two of them stood there looking at me. I supported my foot on the bumper, tried again, tugging harder. It's tough, they said. They said: That's enough! They said: Stop! I looked at Robinson; he was pale. He asked if I was OK; he couldn't have been OK himself. Everything's fine. I want to get that carburetor out of there and I'm going to, all right? My shoe slipped, I slid, and when I got up off the floor my body had changed. My pulse and breathing were fast, I had a dry mouth and a cold feeling in my stomach, my hands were trembling. I'm going to get this piece of shit out of there, I said. I leaned over the engine, used every muscle in my body, every bit of will to yank the carburetor from the car. I couldn't. I've got more experience at it, get out of the way, they said. I kicked the car's body. Even if I have to bang the shit out of it, I said. Marcão pulled me away: You're not going to bang the shit out of anything. It's my car. Just look what you did to the door. I saw a knife on the table and yelled for Robinson to get me out of there.

On the sidewalk, my cousin gripped both my hands in his: What's wrong with you, man? It's just a carburetor. It's just a car. That's Marcão, your friend. Have you gone crazy?

You got any dough you can lend me, Robinson? Money to lend you? Shit, Máiquel, I'm unemployed. I've got to look out for myself. What about Marcão? I don't know about Marcão. I already owe him, I can't ask for anymore. If you want to, go talk to him.

I took the photo of Ezequiel out of my pocket. You know this guy? No. What do you want with him? I'm going to kill him. You're going to kill that guy? Robinson asked a lot of things; he was startled. It made no difference to me.

I still wasn't sure I was going to kill Ezequiel. I shouldn't have said anything. I said something because I was mad at Marcão and Robinson. I said it because I didn't have anything else to say.

As I was going into Gonzaga's, a man in a white Opala

honked at me. He waved. I don't know who it was. After I killed Suel, people did that kind of thing.

You know this guy? Gonzaga took a long look at Ezequiel's photo. It's easy to find out, he said. Leave the picture with me. I went and played pool till nightfall, my thoughts dropping into the pockets. A lot.

That night I made Gorby get into the shower with me. Pink all over, fattening. Are you hungry, you little rascal? I fried some eggs, made rice, washed the dishes, swept the kitchen. Bad thoughts tried to intrude, but I didn't let them. Cledir, Cledir, Cledir. It would be nice if she showed up. I would suck her breasts, her throat, her groin, her juice. I'd show her how waves are created. Horses. How two parts fit together. I wanted very much to speak to Cledir. I wanted to explain. I had always exaggerated in sex because women taught me it was necessary to exaggerate. Ask them what they want and they say: Fuck me. Make my heart ache. Make me scream. Do something. They say: Squeeze the fruit and take the juice. That's how it is. Women like troops, horses, lances, things that invade and conquer. Things that dominate and bring peace. Things that occupy and leave marks behind. Women. Cledir, forgive me.

The man to kill; the thoughts came like sheep and I let them jump the fences. They jumped. Things became clear; I was lining everything up. I would kill Ezequiel because it was important to me. Good teeth, gift horse, hunting. There was no reason to be afraid. I just had to do things calmly, plan ahead. It wouldn't be hard to find out where he lived. His habits. Schedules. The target. Ezequiel must frequent some bar; he'd return home by himself, walking down a deserted street. A shot in the back; Marcão would lend me a car. No one would see, I wouldn't get caught. I'd throw the weapon in the river, and that would be that. I'd make my peace with Cledir, get a job and marry her. I'd have children, a normal life. And I'd never again do coke either. That stuff about being cold-blooded is all wrong. A man's blood should have a temperature of ninety-eight point six degrees.

Rapist. Goat-footed, coarse temperaments / raping hamadryad virgins. Fifth grade, Dona Leda's Portuguese class. The most beautiful thing in the world was to hear Dona Leda reading poetry, her deep blue eyes. Once I asked if she was the one who wrote those things and she said no, it was a very important man. My God, poetry is like a cathedral, and I never feel clean enough in a cathedral. I memorized some verses to please Dona Leda and sometimes, out of nowhere, they come dancing into my mind. Hamadryads. I left school and today I don't consider myself worthy of entering its gates, but say a word and I'll be saved.

Goat-footed, coarse temperaments / raping hamadryad virgins. Poetry. Ezequiel was a rapist, they said. Everybody had something to tell me about Ezequiel. He raped a student. Raped a blonde woman. Raped a woman who worked in a bank. Raped a housewife. I raped a Mappin salesgirl.

It was no trouble at all finding out about Ezequiel's life. All I did was stay at home, receiving, listening. Just that. The information would come in. Address, place of work, police record, victims, dramas. They spoon-fed me. Gonzaga taped Ezequiel's photo over the counter in the bar, and every day somebody would leave something for me. Letters, money, offers of help, supplies, friends. Robinson told Marcão that I was going to kill Ezequiel. Marcão told the entire neighborhood. Everybody knew.

Sometimes I would go to Mappin. Cledir refused to speak

to me. The first time she saw me she ran like crazy toward the bus stop, with me close behind. A cop stopped me, asked for my ID. She got on the first Vila Olímpia–Lapa bus and rode past me without looking, while the policeman frisked me. Another time, she threatened to scream if I didn't leave her alone. She changed her work schedule. She got a transfer to another branch, thinking I wouldn't find her, but I did. The downtown Mappin, across from the Municipal Theater. When I didn't have anything to do I'd go there, wait in the shoe section, looking at moccasins. That was all.

I followed Ezequiel, learned everything there was to know about him. Twice a week I went to Dr Carvalho's. He asked how things were going. Fine, I said.

Sometimes I'd think about Suel's girlfriend. Sometimes I'd go to the movies to see Loves of a Scoundrel, Nymphette Island Orgy, How to Avoid Divorce. Sometimes I stayed home with Gorby, reading the newspaper. Carlos Otávio Feres, ninety-six. Survived by children and grandchildren. Vila Alpina Crematorium.

One night, coming back drunk from Gonzaga's bar, I saw the living-room light was on at my place. The door opened and there she was. I crossed the street at a run, but she was faster and locked the door. I was trying to break it down when the thought hit me that it might be a trap. There might be others in there, friends of Suel's. I was frightened, wanted to run. My legs took a couple of steps backward; I tripped and fell into the rose bed. I'd never seen those roses. The door opened again; I was on the ground. I closed my eyes and felt like praying. The smell of roses. For the love of God, don't kill me. Everybody says things like that at the moment of death. They think they can inspire pity. They can't. There were no shots. I opened my eyes. She was standing there.

It takes me a long time to understand things. It's like there's some kind of veil covering my understanding. She was trembling, I was trembling too. She was by herself. It wasn't any kind of trap. There was no revenge, nothing. She was just a girl. Suel's girlfriend. I'd finally found her.

6

S he told me:
 My home was an orange-colored truck, and my father painted on the bumper: I'm ugly and live far away. Pará, Bahia, Pernambuco, Minas Gerais, Paraná, you can't imagine the beautiful places I've seen. My life was on the road. He used to say I was the most important thing in the world and would take me everywhere, from the time I was two years old and my mother died. I remember a pink church in the middle of the woods, such a romantic place. I saw a field of sunflowers. I saw people dying. I saw buffalo. I saw Indians. I saw gold. We ate at filling stations, slept in the cab; sometimes we'd stop at a hotel, depending on the cargo. Stone, sand, bricks, my father hauled everything, everything and everywhere, as long as they paid. If there was a river or a beach along the road, we'd swim. If there was a celebration in some town, we'd dance. He taught me to read and write. You can dictate anything you like, I'll write it down. I can do figures too. Did I tell you my name is Érica? Everybody likes my name. Some places are dull, you

go there and there's nothing: cows and sun, that's all. Of all the cities I've seen, Rio de Janeiro is the prettiest. And the one with the most crazies is São Paulo. It was in São Paulo that I met my true love. He gave me these sneakers, my true love. We were going to get married, wedding gown and all, and spend our honeymoon in a house by the beach. I love the beach. We hadn't set a date, but that was my dream. The husband's the one who has to work, Suel used to say. I don't know how to do anything. I'm fifteen and I've never worked; Suel took care of me. Suel told me never to go to the police. I'm afraid of the police. Jennifer, my friend, said I should turn you in. So did Suel's mother. She threw me out of the house. We lived there, Suel and me. Now my life is shit. I'm going to stay here, in your house; I'm going to live here. It won't do any good to order me out; I won't go. If you put me out on the street I'll stay on the sidewalk and every time you leave I'll find a way in. You have to take care of me. You have to put up with me. You have to provide me with food, clothes, whatever I need. If you hadn't killed Suel I'd be with him. You turned my heart into a pile of rocks. Suel was my true love and you fucked me. That's what I came to say and I've said it.

7

I had my mouth open. Dr Carvalho had a small electric drill in his hand. If it hurts, let me know. It hurt already, but it was another kind of pain. I don't know what a criminal's soul is like, but the soul of an honest man, a good man, is a hell. Dr Carvalho had read that somewhere. How interesting, think about it, he said. I thought. Any man's soul is a hell, my soul is a hell, Érica's. She cried before falling asleep. A hell, Dr Carvalho said. Just go for a walk around here, know what you'll find? You'll find iron bars. Walls. Barbed wire. Broken glass, that's what you'll find around here. You'll find alarm systems. Armored doors. Steel. That's right, trenches. All we think about is defending ourselves. Pillboxes. That's how we live, he continued. It's true, I thought: bars, walls, broken glass. I have all of that inside me: stone, mud, tigers in my heart. Traffic lights: who stops at traffic lights? We don't stop at lights, he said. Our souls are a hell. We don't tip. We don't open our windows. We don't look to the side. We don't look behind. We don't leave our houses. We're afraid. Panic. We're restive. We have hate in our hearts. Our souls are a hell.

It had nothing to do with Dr Carvalho, but I didn't feel comfortable in that office. The white clothes, the smell of cleaning products, order, the buttons to control things; all of that wasn't for me. He displayed his ideas, smiled, worked on my teeth, but I didn't feel comfortable. I understood everything: the world is shit, our souls are a hell. It's all true, broken glass, but what could I say? That's exactly the way it was. Or not; what difference does it make?

Besides which, my mind was occupied. Érica. I spent the night in the living room while she slept in my bed. Fifteen years old. Every woman I like has eyes like hers, eyes that scream. Érica cried before she fell asleep; I could hear her sobs. She must have been missing Suel. It must be good to have a woman who cries for you before she goes to sleep. I decided I would take care of Érica. My hands would take away her pain. That's what I would do.

Dr Carvalho handed me a mirror so that I could see the filled tooth. In place of the hole was a grayish material. Very nice. If he hadn't been standing beside me I'd have laughed out loud like that guy in the whiskey commercials. I like that guy, with his pleated pants, that blonde that he keeps kissing. I like the house, the music, the party, people drinking and enjoying themselves, and me without a penny, a pile of bad checks: your name is mud around here, they told me. I asked what was going to happen to me. You can't use your charge account anymore. Paying by installment, buying property, shopping in department stores, none of that. Your name is on the Central Bank's blacklist.

We went into the small room to the side. Dr Carvalho smiled; I could see his canines clearly. Well?

He wanted me to open the sewer. It happens that at the time I still hadn't learned to hate. They could say whatever they wanted about Ezequiel and all I managed to see in front of me was a poor devil. Ezequiel seemed like a stray dog: skinny, melancholy, with the hungry look of a street mongrel. He worked in a pet shop, an honest job selling rabbits, white mice, parakeets. Selling birdseed, pet food, cages. I never saw anything strange about Ezequiel. He went to work early, did his job, returned home, watched TV, swept the sidewalk, that's it. I never saw Ezequiel drink, smoke or carouse with women. He didn't play soccer, pool or cards, didn't dance on Sunday or go to Mass. He stayed home with his mother, a good, hard-working lady. Everything normal, except his look, a look that saw everything and nothing at all, like those guys in Da Sé Square who pretend to be blind. I don't know if he raped a lot of women; maybe he did. People say he did. He raped a little blonde girl. A decent older woman. A woman who sells popcorn. A tramp. So what? What did that have to do with me? If Ezequiel went around fucking women, it wasn't my problem. I didn't feel hatred. Dr Carvalho wanted me to hate Ezequiel, but I didn't hate him. My heart was free.

Every person in the neighborhood brought me a chunk of hate to swallow: the way Ezequiel attacked women from behind, grabbing their wrists, forcing them to get down on all fours, pointing kitchen knives, pocket knives, beating, hurting, cutting, spitting in their pussies. I swallowed all that and didn't feel anything. But when Dr Carvalho asked me about developments I simply turned my back on myself, left myself talking to no one. It's all set up, I said, all that's left is to buy the revolver. Dr Carvalho gave me money. Buy whatever you have to; get this over with as soon as possible.

Dr Carvalho wasn't my boss, but I obeyed because he was

a good, honest man and he was keeping his part of the deal, to fill my rotten teeth.

When I got home I heard Érica's voice in the yard. She was sitting in the doorway feeding breadcrumbs to the pig. He's hungry, she said. Érica ran her hands along Gorby's rolls of fat as if she liked him. I went to the kitchen, got water from the fridge. Érica came after me, sat on the table, swinging her legs. Nice legs. Nice arms.

Why did you kill Suel?

I pretended not to hear and went into the bathroom. I opened my zipper; Érica pushed on the door and leaned against the jamb. I got irritated. Get out of here, goddammit! I'm not looking, she said. I don't care if you're not looking, close that goddamn door. She closed it, I finished pissing, came out, she was still there, standing in my way. Suel never did anything to you. Why did you kill Suel? Fucking shit, I said. You can stay here, you can sleep in my bed, you can eat my food, wear my clothes, spend my money, but don't jerk my chain, you hear? That's all I said, just that. We were standing there facing each other and she pushed me aside and went into the bedroom, slamming the door.

Don't slam the door, I shouted.

I felt like going into her room, shaking her by the shoulders. You bitch, don't ever slam the door in my house again, understand?

Ten minutes later, at the bus stop, I saw Érica running like a young goat trying to catch me. Wait, she said. I paid no attention, got on the bus as it was leaving; she wouldn't make it. I paid the fare, sat down near the driver, and immediately afterwards she sat down beside me. Pay the guy the fare, she said. What guy? The collector. I got up, paid Érica's fare, and returned. She was wearing a loose T-shirt with a pink flower design. Her small breasts were free inside there. I sensed Érica's smell, her breath, saw her long fingers, the shape of her nails, her thighs. It bothered me. Érica was only fifteen, she was a widow; I didn't want anything to do with her. Cledir was the woman for me, not Érica. We rode by a store that sold construction materials. A hypermarket. A housing project. A circus. Do you like circuses? Yes, I said. I don't, I think they're a drag. I never found circus clowns the least bit funny, even when I was a kid. I think circuses are ridiculous, I hate them. I like the movies. What I like most is going to the movies, sitting there in the dark thinking that the story is happening to me. Suel liked them too. He had a pal who worked at the ticket booth at the Copan; we saw a lot of movies for free.

I felt anger toward Suel, anger because he liked movies, anger because he had a friend at the ticket booth. Taking Érica to the Copan, that faggot, that tape-player thief, that black son of a bitch! Where are we going now? I said I had an appointment and would rather go by myself. This street reminds me of the Avenida Brasil. Do you know Rio de Janeiro? No, I said. I didn't feel like talking. It's great. Look into my eyes. I didn't look. When it rains in Rio de Janeiro, the sea turns the color of my eyes, swear to God. I still didn't look. I took out a fiver, gave it to Érica, got off the bus.

The Cruzeiro do Sul shantytown was near the airport. Nobody drove a car in there because the only access road was full of speed bumps, like a bobsled. The best thing was to use the pedestrian overpass that crossed the Trabalhadores highway. That's what I did. I walked past a lot of shacks, lots of For Sale signs, everybody wanting to get out of there.

I felt a bad sensation, somebody behind me. I looked round

43

and there she was, Érica. I don't know how to get back, she said. I don't know my way around here. Where are we? It was good to know that Érica was following me, but I sighed, putting on an expression of annoyance. I walked on, with her behind me. Look at that, she said, soing done. Sewing is s-e-w, not s-o, she said, laughing. Érica is very dumb. I came to the junkyard, told them to get Big Buck, I'm Robinson's cousin. I didn't know the first thing about weapons. Buck talked about AR-15s, HK machine guns, 9mm handguns, Winchesters, repeating pump models, Ruger rifles, the Vietnam war, the works. He showed me a pretty weapon. This one here, my man, will splatter even a cow against the wall. You gonna take it? I want something more ordinary, like the ones everybody uses. He handed me a Taurus .38. Érica asked to hold it, then pointed the barrel at me. Have you got a bullet? she asked. Buck laughed. I laughed. She pulled the trigger, aiming at my head. I paid, and we left.

On the bus, Érica asked what I had felt when I held the gun. I didn't feel anything, I said. That was a lie; I'd felt anxious, a chill. I didn't like weapons. Holding a gun is like pulling on a pair of boots, she said. Or putting a crown on your head. It changes everything. Did you ever put a crown on your head? I asked. No, she said. We laughed. She turned serious and said that holding a revolver was exactly that, wearing boots and a crown.

The bus broke down when we were nearly home, on 7th Street. We got out and she wanted to walk. We did. Why did you buy a gun? Shops, 3 1/2″×5″ photos in five minutes. To defend myself. Tiger Real Estate. Is there somebody who wants to kill you? Yes, I lied. Érica wanted strawberry ice cream. A street vendor was selling bandeaux; she tried on several, said the red one was the prettiest, and asked me to buy it. I bought the blue one too. She saw a cloth shoe. It's a slipper, she said, buy it for me. I still had some money, so I bought it. Érica liked trinkets, she was happy, and I was happy too. It was good to wander around there.

When we crossed the street I took her hand. A small, soft hand. Érica pulled away and said she wasn't stupid. I can cross the street by myself, she said.

The next day, I went to the pet shop. My idea was to wait till nightfall when Ezequiel left. I would follow him and kill him. I wanted to shoot him in the back; he'd be walking along and suddenly, bang, bang, bang, he wouldn't be walking anymore. Ezequiel wasn't in the shop, which bothered me. I went in. There wasn't a salesclerk in sight. I stood there looking at the little blue chicks. What stupidity, dyeing the poor things. Can I help you? Ezequiel popped up suddenly from someplace, maybe from the sidewalk. Is there anything you'd like? A delicate way of serving the customer, a good guy, Ezequiel. A toucan, I said. We don't sell toucans, it's against the law. Thanks, I said. I went to the lunch counter on the corner and spent the day there, studying. Selling rabbits. I needed to find a job. After I'd killed Ezequiel, I thought, they'd need a clerk.

At six o'clock Ezequiel left work, caught the Vila Ida bus, got off at the stop by the bakery, bought bread, stopped by the pool room and watched the game for a while. I screwed up, he saw me, I hid behind a huge black guy. Ezequiel stretched his neck, looked for me, then gave up. At seven-thirty he left the bakery and went down Flores Street. He walked slowly, the bread under his arm. Men think crazy things while they walk. Ezequiel, a rapist. Goat-footed, coarse temperaments, etc. The street was busy, people leaving from work, filling the spaces, the crowds. I had the weapon ready in the pocket of my jacket, waiting for the ideal moment.

He would turn the corner, and that's where it would be, on the street where he lived. Ezequiel stopped in front of a luggage shop. He looked in the window. Two salesgirls talking, laughing; he liked them. Clearance, don't miss it.

After we passed the bus stop, Ezequiel turned into a deserted street and slowed down. Suddenly he stopped, looked back and saw me. He walked toward me, calmly. No one was around. You want to talk to me? he asked. Yes. He smiled, a polite smile. What can I do for you? I pulled out the gun, took aim, and bang. I missed him with the first shot. What's going on? A sincere question, he didn't understand what was happening. What was happening was a gun. Bang. I missed a second time. The third one caught him in the thigh, the fourth one in the chest. He fell; I missed with two more shots. Ezequiel was still alive, moaning, suffering, trying to get up, to say something, he wanted to go home to his mother. I was out of bullets. He couldn't remain alive, not now. I yanked a piece of wood from a fence around a tree and threw myself on him. I hit him in the head, hammered at him, hammered, put out his eyes. Ezequiel was still alive, my arms ached, I rammed the wooden spike into the rapist's heart. I'd seen this on television, the hero killing the vampire. Ezequiel vomited blood and died.

I crossed the street and got out of there.

When I opened the door at home I saw Érica and Cledir sitting on the sofa, giggling.

8

Prison inmate smokes crack to celebrate victory.

The first-place winner in the anti-drug essay contest at Moreira Aguiar Prison received three hundred packs of cigarettes as a prize and celebrated the victory by spending the entire week consuming crack.

The volume of the television was high; you could hear the news from the bathroom. Voices too. Érica laughed at the item. Crack, the drain, I soaped myself, water, showered, rinsed off. I wanted to calm down before talking to Cledir. Missing four shots. I was irritated. All wrong, what stupidity. Ezequiel could have died without knowing what hit him, with dignity. Dying isn't a problem. The terrible part is when death makes you count down, ten, nine, eight, seven, six, five, incurable diseases, planes with broken engines, four, three, two, falling, falling, falling, till you hit the sea and explode; that's what I did to Ezequiel. I screwed up; that's how it had been my entire life, screwing up, leaving things half finished, doing things wrong, screwing up. I never learned math. Or chemistry. I never understood the words they use

47

in newspapers. They used to draw donkey ears on the cover of my notebooks while I watched the children eating their snacks at recess.

Érica knocked on the door. You've been in there for half an hour.

When I came out, Cledir said she had to talk to me. Outside, she said.

There was a VW van in front of the house. I leaned against it and waited for Cledir to speak. I wanted so much for Cledir to forgive me, and she'd come to forgive me on that very day, a rotten day for forgiveness. I should have dried my hair better; water was running down the back of my neck, wetting my shirt collar. I have two important things to tell you: the first is that I love you. The second is that you're a miserable son of a bitch, she said. I'm pregnant, pregnant, Máiquel. You're an idiot, an imbecile, that's what you are. I wanted to be your wife, make love to you, I wanted to tell you I loved you, that the two of us could build a life together, with me working, you working, have children, buy a house, go to Santos on vacation, get the family together on Sundays, have a normal life like everybody else, but you had to go and ruin everything. You had to hurt me, throw me on the floor and rape me, 'cause that's what it was, a rape, forced intercourse. I've always dreamed about having a wonderful life. I was a virgin. I wished I could fall in love with Odair. Odair works at the savings and loan. Odair bought a small house, Odair likes me, Odair likes barbecue, Odair is the stay-at-home type, Odair has Keds, Odair wants to be a father, Odair believes in God, Odair would make a good husband. Odair, Odair, Odair. But you had to show up at Mappin to buy some clothes, you had to tell me that life without love was very sad. You had to ruin everything. Now I'm in this shitty situation. I'm pregnant, did you hear

48

me? It's your child, so now what? Are you just going to stand there? Say something, Máiquel.

I had just killed a man and Cledir was pregnant. Say something, she said, for God's sake say something. Let's get married, I said. She stopped crying. Is that what you want?

Érica opened the living-room door, put the trash outside, dancing, the music at full volume, and smiled at us: I gestured for her to come in, she raised her arms, showing a band of belly between her T-shirt and her shorts, the navel, her body dancing, twisting, kidding around for our benefit. I smiled; Cledir's jaw dropped. Érica disappeared, but we could still hear her voice. Let's have a talk with your mother, I said, get married. We made a lot of plans, even though I felt like a pipe had burst inside me.

I took my future wife away and ran back home; Érica needed to hear the news as soon as possible. I didn't want her to feel unprotected; after all, nothing would change, or at least I wanted to think nothing would change. Cledir had to agree. There would be a room just for Érica in our house, a room I'd build myself, with a comfortable bed full of pillows. Érica could go to school if she wanted to. Wasn't she all the time saying that she wanted to know more about geoscience, about how things happen on the planet: rain, hurricanes, earthquakes? Dandy. None of that had anything to do with me getting married, but it was a way of making Érica happy.

I was going to tell her, I'd made up my mind. Except that when she was feeling sad, or threatened, inept, frustrated, or even when she was full of happiness, Érica would release a locomotive from her chest, a locomotive that ran after you, ran over you, crushed you, turned you into a frightened bloody pulp. I wanted to talk to her about my marriage, my child that was going to be born, but there came Érica's train, whistling, gathering steam, running over people, showing me a pile of jars, creams, mixing sticks, envelopes. We're going to dye your hair, retouch the roots, she said. I didn't feel the least bit like it. I was sad, very sad, but there wasn't any choice, I was already a passenger on Érica's train. Do this, do that, fetch the comb, hold your head this way, do that, fetch the comb, fetch the comb, fetch the comb.

An hour later, my scalp burnt terribly. We went to the bathroom, I sat in my undershorts, she soaped my head, her leg resting against mine, her chest on my shoulder, her breathing, the smell of her hair, the lions, the thunder, the hurricanes, everything burned inside and outside of me.

I was pleased to look at myself in the mirror and see that I was blonder than the first time. You like it? I like it a lot, I said. Then say this: bitch-in', just like that, slowly. It's slang that everybody's using. It means great, fantastic, awesome. Bitch-in', I said. We were so close that I felt like kissing Érica. I like you like that, she said, blond.

Máiquel, somebody called from outside.

We went out. Robinson and Marcão were in a metallic-brown Dodge Dart, chewing gum. You're really off the wall, man. Everybody's waiting for you. They all want to throw their arms around you. We're going to celebrate. Celebrate what? Érica asked. I didn't want to take Érica, didn't want to say I'd killed a man, another man, but she got into Marcão's car without waiting to be asked. Is this a Dodge Dart? Érica got enchanted by cars, Érica got enchanted by anything. Wow, a Dodge Dart. Robinson offered coke; I wasn't going to accept, Érica was only fifteen. But before I could say no, she was already snorting. I love coke, I love grass, I love gin, I love crack, she said, very excited.

I snorted too, and this time it was different: something exploded inside me and it was a spectacular explosion. Blood rushed in and out of my heart, air rushed in and out of my lungs, I forgot that I had killed a goat-foot, forgot my destiny of screwing up, forgot that Cledir was pregnant, forgot everything and just thought about feeling good.

At the intersection of Santo Amaro with Juscelino Kubitschek two guys were changing the tire of a red Beetle. I put my head out the window: Fuck you, faggots! That was real funny, Érica enjoyed the joke. We started messing with everybody, cursing, sons of bitches, cuckold, whore, slut, come suck me, lady. Marcão got with the scene too and drove faster, ignoring stoplights, nearly sideswiping the suckers, scaring pedestrians. Everything was like that, wonderful. It was one of those magical moments in life, us in the Dodge Dart, the world out there was ours, when suddenly some fool, a poor devil of a drunk, got in our way and crash! He flipped in the air and was squashed against the road. The son of a bitch had ruined everything. We got out. Robinson felt for the beggar's pulse. No pulse. He's dead, Robinson screamed. Shit, we killed the guy, we killed the guy, we're in deep shit. There were sobs in Robinson's voice. He walked around the drunk, hysterical. Marcão also panicked: Let's take him to the hospital. We're not taking him anywhere, I said, he's dead. Can't you see that? Érica watched us from inside the car. It wasn't our fault, I said, it wasn't anybody's fault. Guys like that get drunk, try to cross the street, shit, it's not our fault. I looked around: nobody. Start the car, Marcão, and let's get out of here. We left a trail of burning rubber, without looking back.

Nobody said anything. Marcão kept popping his gum like he always did when he was nervous. Robinson was shaking.

Where are we going? Érica asked. I killed a man, Érica. A rapist. We're going to celebrate. I didn't look at her face, I didn't want to know Érica's opinion. I'd killed a guy, run over a drunk, that's just who I was. My tooth was filled and I didn't care what Érica thought. If she went along with it, fine; if she didn't, she could pack her bags and bye-bye. Turn up the volume, Robinson. Robinson turned up the volume and I sang loudly until we got to Gonzaga's. I don't know if she had anything to say.

They were giving a party for me. Gonzaga offered beer on the house; Manuel, the butcher, brought a sirloin. Let's slice it, fry it, roast it. Congratulations, congratulations, they kept saying over and over. Robinson and Marcão looked like they'd seen a ghost, until the alcohol started taking effect. When the news came on the radio Gonzaga turned up the volume: a couple less criminals running around. Santo Amaro rapist clubbed to death! That's how it should be, Máiquel, congratulations, criminals have to get screwed! They were happy, they lined up to say hello, and it didn't seem like a Western movie to me. A guy said he was walking down the street when I killed Ezequiel. I saw the whole thing, I'll tell you what happened. The audience enjoyed the part where I hammered him on the head and poked out Ezequiel's eyes. Those who were mothers loved it, and I thought it natural that they would. The gifts were even better than when I killed Suel: binoculars, ten pounds of rice, a chunk of rump roast, a deck of cards, sunglasses, T-shirts, along with a lot of silly stuff.

We kept going to the john to snort. Érica was real crazy, and Zé Onofre wouldn't leave her side. Let's get out of here, I said.

We walked to Sete de Abril Street and went into the movie

theater. On the screen a blonde woman, hooked on crack, was telling her boyfriend: vampires are luckier than we are. They can feed off others; we have to feed on ourselves.

When we left the theater, the euphoria from the coke had faded, along with that entire magic feeling. We went to a bar nearby, ordered vodka. Érica asked me if that was my profession, killing people. Of course not, I said. What about that guy we ran over? What's that got to do with anything? Didn't you feel sorry for him? Sure I did, but it was Marcão's fault, didn't you see how he drives? You could have agreed to take him to the hospital. Yeah, right, I said. You know what would've happened there? They'd have seen we were high on drugs, they'd have seen that Marcão's car was hot, and we'd go to jail. You want to go to jail? That Dodge Dart is hot? she asked. I don't know, but I suspect. Marcão, I don't know, I just don't know, but it could be hot, that's what I meant.

They were playing a song in English that had the word love in it over and over. Érica said she wanted to dance. Here? This wasn't a night club, it was a bar where you drank at the counter. So what? We began to dance. A woman looked at us, Érica got irritated. What's your problem? You want your face rearranged? I pulled her closer to me. Let it go, I said. I pressed my body against hers. Cotton candy, I knew, was about to envelop us, and that's exactly what happened. The cotton candy did envelop us; we swirled and swirled and swirled. That girl, Cledir, is she your girlfriend? She's a friend, I said. What did she want? Money, I said. Her mother's going to have an operation, she needs money. I stuck my nose up against Érica's neck and we continued like that, turning, turning; people sleeping, waking up, going to work and the two of us turning.

We went home on foot, Érica playing at keeping her balance on the curbs. When she came close to falling, I would wrap her in my arms. It was good.

At home, she went straight to the bedroom. Help me get this shoe off, she said. I unbuckled her sandal, kissed her ankles, heels, she pulled me by the hair, fuck me, she said, fuck me, and she grabbed my prick, and when she did that I felt a kind of stab in the heart, a good kind of stab. Believe me, there is such a thing.

Her body was the most beautiful thing in the world: the lower part of her calf, all the area around her navel, the bristly hair of her thighs, her sweet true poetic eyes. I was ready to invade, conquer, tear away, leave marks. She was ready to be divided in half, two Éricas; an ocean would come from my body. It was then that something inside me, a sea monster, an enemy submarine, rose up and said: That girl, Cledir, is my fiancée, I'm going to marry her.

Érica didn't push me away; she just made me get off her. She stood up, put on her clothes. You can sleep here if you want to. I'm sleeping on the sofa tonight, she said.

9

I left through my bedroom window so as not to run into Érica and went to the Park of White Waters, a pretty place. The sun was shining, the ice-cream vendor had his radio on, a great time for you to get a job with the Tax Department, two thousand openings for high-school graduates. I stretched out on a bench and looked at the trees, not thinking about anything. Human beings think too much, that's the problem. People oughtn't to think so much in my opinion. They ought to love and work. They ought to get some sun and look at the trees. When my head feels like thinking, I buy some gum and chew, chew hard; gum helps me not think. Sometimes thoughts try to creep in, try to build a tower, stone by stone, force their way into a person's head, but people are stronger than thoughts, people can forget. And when they can't forget, they can sing Tim Maia songs.

Reality lies, that's how I sometimes feel. Something outside of me telling lies, making up things to deceive me; that's how it was that day, but I didn't let it get to me. I chewed gum and sang and let time go by.

At six I went to Cledir's house; I had agreed to speak to her mother. She opened the door and kissed me on the mouth, a good kiss, it's good to kiss. Look how it's grown, Cledir said, putting my hand on her belly. She didn't have a belly, but I said it had really grown. My mother is on her way, Cledir said, she's getting ready. First we'll talk about marriage and then about the pregnancy. I agreed with everything. We sat on the sofa, holding hands. She asked if I was nervous; I said no. Cledir led me to the refrigerator and showed me bottles of beer and a chocolate cake. My mother bought it for us to celebrate the engagement.

When we went back to the living room, Dona Irene was already there. We shook hands, sat down. Cledir prepared the terrain; all I had to do was come in with the tractor. But something wasn't working right. I couldn't speak; they stared at me. The girl sitting in front of me was the kind of girl to be loved, the best thing in my life, and the man was me, a lucky guy. So what's the problem, man? Do what you have to do, I thought. I wanted to ask Cledir to marry me, but my eyes were glued to a picture beside the window, Christ on a cross in space, falling into the sea, the sea that was also the planet Earth. I remembered a movie I'd seen with Érica: a cop with crack in his bloodstream sees Christ and asks, What is it, man? You want to tell me something? The two of them looked at me, two decent women, holding hands, the house smelling of wax, the furniture free of dust, the beds made, the chocolate cake, the beer, the scrubbed pans, the Formica cabinets. I started crying right there in front of them.

Cledir pulled me out of the house. What's going on? It had nothing to do with Cledir, or with Érica, nothing to do with the child that was going to be born, with marriage, nothing. It had to do with my gaps. I wasn't the man for Cledir. We stood there, leaning against the gate, Cledir very upset. I smoked, inhaling, thinking, ideas coming into my head. When I finished the cigarette, I knew what to do.

Cledir, I'm not going to get married. You can get an abortion, lots of women do that. You can have the baby, and I'll help with the dough. Getting married won't work. It won't work because I don't want to. If you want an explanation, I'm not going to explain anything. It doesn't do any good to explain.

That's what I wanted to say, but before I could begin, we heard the sound of breaking glass. We ran inside and found Cledir's mother collapsed on the table in the middle of the living room.

When we got to the emergency room she was already dead. Heart attack, said the medic on duty. Cledir clung to me and sobbed. Yes, I would get married. And I'd buy the coffin too, spend the night at the wake, go to the funeral, do everything a man ought to do. I did, I went ahead and did the things, that's what I did. I went to the morgue, helped dress the body, bought flowers, saw to the grave, spoke with gravediggers, chose the coffin, sent word to friends, prayed the prayers, and dried Cledir's tears.

The next day, after the funeral, we talked about the future. We'd get married on Saturday. There wouldn't be any party because we were unhappy, just a cake for the best man and maid of honor. We'd live in her house and Érica would come with me; Cledir didn't mind.

Cledir was afraid to sleep alone; she wanted me to stay. But I hadn't been home for two days. Besides which, I had an important appointment that night, one I couldn't miss.

★   ★   ★

Dr Carvalho's house had a lot of mahogany and satin, a Chinese fan, lacquer, colorful plumes in gigantic vases, and rugs that came halfway up your calves, a type of interior decoration that, months later, when I started making money, I found out was just like luxury motels in São Paulo.

I was happy about being invited, but I was enormously uneasy; coffee, amphetamines, it seemed like I'd drunk too much coffee. I was in a hurry, disturbed, I wanted the dinner to be over as soon as possible, wanted to go home. That's how I am; there are things I don't like to experience, to go through. I like it when they're behind me, I like remembering them.

The situation these days is like an old coat in a cow's mouth, said the fat man sitting at the other end of the table. If you try to pull it out, it'll rip; if you leave it alone, the cow'll eat it. Absolutely right, said Dr Carvalho, that's exactly how it is. I read in the paper the other day a story that illustrates very well the subject of our conversation: a shop in Miami that sells articles for the pool, one of those things Americans do. They invented tattletale capsules; they're right there in the shop, with ads and everything. You feed your guest a capsule and if he pees in the pool, his urine turns blue. You're thinking, well and good, the Americans have solved the problem of a guy taking a piss in someone else's swimming pool. It so happens that the same shop sells another American invention: pills that neutralize the effect of the tattletale pills. Look what man is capable of: all you have to do is take a neutralizing pill before the tattletale pill and you're golden; you can piss in any pool anywhere without anybody knowing the difference. You laugh. It's true, I read it in the paper. In other words, man always finds a way out.

They laughed a lot, and I found it funny myself. I didn't know that the rich pissed in their friends' pools. We're laughing, but we ought to be crying, said Sílvio, the fat man; his name was Sílvio Dantas. Man is hopeless, and that's sad, said Sílvio, Mr Sílvio, who looked at me more than anyone else round the table when we were having dinner. Only one thing works with man, he said. Only one thing, and everybody knows what it is. Mr Sílvio raised his wineglass and smiled at me, a smile that I was learning to recognize. The cops, the neighbors, the merchants, the housewives, Mr Sílvio and Dr Carvalho; they all smile the same way. Me too. We all laughed.

The tropical pineapple arrived, a kind of salad that's served inside the individual pineapples. I'd never seen it before. What kind of insanity is this? Dr Carvalho asked his wife. A great guy, Dr Carvalho, great and down-to-earth, all the time refilling my wineglass; have some more, relax, he said. Tropical pineapple, my wife invents these things, he said. Drink up. I knew that Dr Carvalho was very pleased with my work. Eat. And I was very pleased with the fillings in my teeth. You've carried out your part well, he said when I arrived. Do you smoke? Dr Carvalho's wife was colder, but she thanked me too. Try these American cigarettes. I saw that she noticed my shitty shoes. American cigarettes are the best in the world. None of the others even come close. She was wearing copper-colored sandals and I tried to hide my shoes, leaving the newspaper on top of them when I sat down on the sofa. Let me have that paper, she said. The children, she said, children make such a mess. My shoes were ugly as shit.

Dr Carvalho's dinner table had a glass top. They didn't use the traditional type of tablecloth, they used American place mats because they're more practical. I couldn't stop looking at the shoes. I pretended to be looking at my plate, but I was looking at the shoes: Dr Carvalho's had a leather tassel, Mr Sílvio's had laces and thick rubber soles, his wife wore kid–leather flats, all of them shined, gleaming, and my shoes looked like they'd spent the night in a toilet. They looked like boats. I sank.

I'm a serious student of every innovation in security systems, said Dr Carvalho. I read specialist publications, test the equipment, so I know what I'm talking about. Anyone for wine? The electronic kind of lock that works with buttons is the safest and the most up–to–date. Dear, where's the corkscrew? As for doors, the most effective is the steel kind they use for safes. They're expensive. I always say, the cost doesn't matter. Life is important. Dear, I think Máiquel would like some more chicken. Alarms and electronic devices, whatever the cost, are cheap. Nowadays there's a whole menu of alarms. Alarms for people who go away to Guarujá for the weekend. Alarms for situations in which the homeowner is overpowered by dangerous criminals. Technically we call them anti–burglary alarms and anti–attack alarms. I've heard that there are also systems that make decisions. For example, by closing the outside door or raising a steel barrier, trapping the criminal somewhere. Electronic stuff. You ask me if any of that works. It's the same story as the tattletale pills and the neutralizing pills. It doesn't solve the problem. Security equipment can improve and offer some help. But if a criminal decides to enter your house, forget all that stuff. He's getting in. He's getting in and he's going to grab your gold, your money, your CD player, your car, and if your daughter's there he's going to take her too. So what's the answer? Buy a pair of geese? Don't laugh, a lot of people do that. A goose is an awful animal, noisy, and will attack any stranger. I'm in favor of it. Walls, dogs, bars, broken glass, carrying a gun. I'm in favor of all of it. Does it do any good? No. Nothing does any good. There's only one thing that solves the problem. Dr Carvalho looked at me, waiting for me to say something. But I didn't have anything to say. I looked at my shoes, listening to the women talk. It's frozen, Gleice comes once a month, and I buy everything. Sirloin, chicken, ground beef, and Gleice makes meals for the entire month, pancakes, meatballs, rolled roast. Gleice cooks very well. I can give you her phone number. I'd never had frozen food. I think it's very good, and the taste is the same. Shall we have the coffee in my office, love?

We went to the office, the men. The women went to the kitchen. On the cream-colored rug my shoes looked even shittier. The softness of the rug emphasized the ugliness of my shoes. I stuck my feet under the table in the middle of the room. It didn't work, I would be blocking the way, so I had no choice. I sat there with them showing, and from time to time Dr Carvalho or Mr Sílvio would look at them, but what could I do? Nothing solves anything. The only thing that works, Dr Carvalho continued, is to do what must be done. And what is it that must be done?

At that moment, Dr Carvalho's daughter came into the office. She was very different from what I had imagined. White boots, a blouse tied at the waist; she looked older than fifteen. Hi, she said to me. Gabriela, please, Dr Carvalho said, we're having a meeting, go back to your room. I had imagined her as a little girl, delicate. My daughter is a flower, Dr Carvalho told me the first time we talked. She was no flower. She was a tree. Érica was a flower. Cledir was a tree. A rubber tree.

What I was saying is this. The main thing is for us not to expect anything from the police. My stomach started to churn inside me. The chicken. I recalled those chickens that rotate on spits. Machines. My stomach turned even more. That's what we have to do, act, Dr Carvalho said. They

61

steal our CD players. They steal our digital watches. They steal our VCRs. Our tape players. They steal our cars. They steal our motorcycles. They steal our wallets. They steal our rings, even our wedding rings. We buy another CD player, another watch, another car and another motorcycle, but we know they're going to steal it. My stomach was like a garbage truck, with the garbage tumbling around inside the drum, stinking. I felt like vomiting. Dr Carvalho was looking at me and then at Mr Sílvio: Don't we have the right to have a store? Is that how it is? Tell me, is that how it is? Have we come that far?

I felt like excusing myself to go to the bathroom, but Mr Sílvio put his hand on my arm: I own a cardboard recycling business, Máiquel. The watchman at my firm was shot to death by those sons of bitches. Know how many times I was held up this month? Six times, can you believe it? Then those sheep-fucking priests come along talking about human rights. Permanent Commission on Human Rights. International Tribunal for Human Rights. They're killing our children, they say. I say: They think like men, they act like men. Our children. Our children are men. Poor and black. A scourge.

My stomach. I was going to vomit. I got up. A scourge.

Máiquel, Mr Sílvio said. I have a proposition for you, Máiquel. Carvalho has told me about your work, Máiquel, he said you're a man to be trusted. I know I can trust you, Máiquel. Look, Máiquel, listen to me, Máiquel, understand something, Máiquel: there's a guy who's making life hell for my business. I even offered him money to stop robbing me, but the kid laughed in my face. I make more from stealing, he told me. You're not about to give me as much as I can steal. Keep your money, he said. Keep it because I'm going to steal it. Look, Máiquel, until that happened I thought it was absurd for somebody to think about killing a person. But now I'll tell you: all I want is to kill the guy. If Santa Claus asked me what I wanted for Christmas, I'd say: to see that guy six feet under. I swear it. That's it. I want that black guy dead. What would it cost for you to kill him?

I couldn't stay there another second. Where's the bathroom, Dr Carvalho? As soon as I closed the door I started vomiting. Vomiting all the chicken with cream sauce, the potatoes, the wine, the tropical pineapple, everything. As I vomited I thought about the money I was going to make if I killed the black guy. I was unemployed. A scourge. I didn't have any money, I needed that money. Blacks. I vomited thinking of what I could buy with that money. Shoes. I vomited everything. Meat. I washed my face. They were in the office, waiting for my answer. Yes or no. Food. An automobile. A watch. Blankets. I sat on the toilet, thinking. I remembered Robinson's father giving my aunt a hard time because of lunch. I wasn't born to cook, she replied. And I wasn't born to sell popcorn, he said. I was born to be president. But till that happens, I try to sell popcorn the best I can. Sell popcorn the best I can, I thought. Or sell pet food. Or sell used cars. Or be a doorman. Or build walls. Those would be the jobs; I'd have to do one of them. Yes or no.

I took a deep breath and opened the door. Gabriela was leaning against the wall in the hallway with an unlit cigarette in her hand. She asked if I had a light. No, I said. She laughed. Her canine teeth were identical to her father's. My father told me what you did to that guy, she said. Brand-new white boots. I thought I had killed Ezequiel because of some other girl, not Gabriela. Hey, man, can't you even say see you later? See you later, I said.

I returned to the office. They were drinking coffee. Here's your coffee, want more sugar? I said no thanks, coffee doesn't agree with me. Do you prefer tea? No, thanks. Coca-Cola? No, I don't want anything. So, Máiquel, what do you think of my offer?

Thank you very much, but I'm not going to kill anybody.

I was feeling better; it had done me good to vomit. I walked home, thinking: I was going to marry Cledir, get a job, take care of Érica. Érica was going to study to be a teacher, or a doctor if she wanted to. Everything was going to work out. My life was going to be good and I wouldn't have to go out there and kill people.

While I walked and looked at my shitty shoes, I thought how funny life was. It runs on its own, like a river, if you let it. Or if you can put a bridle on it and make life your horse. People make of life whatever they want. Each one chooses his fate: his horse or his river.

IO

The best of Patty Pravo, side 1. Qui e là, Oggi qui, Domani là, la ra la la ra ra là. Clapping makes the rhythm, she said, clap your hands, clap, clap, and three and four and sideways and sideways, left and sideways and sideways, forward and two, back, the same, let's go, Robinson, again and sideways. Cledir's feet ruled the dance and clap and four; she didn't know how to dance but she was happy. Let's dance, she said, clapping her hands, laughing loudly, and clap and they took a wrong step and clap, Robinson and Marcão couldn't do anything right and they laughed, and sideways and sideways and when Robinson and Marcão started getting it right she would change the rules and forward, forward, what the shit kind of dance is that, Marcão asked, go ahead, don't talk, she said, and clap and back and back. She's making it up as she goes along, Robinson, she's changed. I haven't changed at all, she said. They laughed and clap and clap, the three people I loved most in the world dancing and laughing at my wedding party and three and four and your attention everybody, Cledir said, turning down the music, attention, the cake. A white light, there wasn't any white light but that's how I felt, a white light on my blazer, on all of us, a white light pouring out milk, peace, Ken and Barbie in wedding outfits on top of the cake, Robinson's mother said Cledir and I had to make a wish when we cut the first slice. Cledir looked pretty, her hair in a bun, a short veil, the ring on her finger. I placed my hand over hers; her neckline showed part of her breasts. I closed my eyes, made my wish, to be a normal man, a man who works and loves his wife and children, that's what I wished for. Cledir cut the cake, Marcão opened the champagne. I don't like champagne, I like beer. Champagne is too sweet, but today is a special day; you're going to have some champagne, yes you are. Robinson's father had a camera in his hand. Come over here, Cledir; Marcão, hand her a glass. We interlaced our arms, each holding his own glass, smiled and click and clap and clap.

Besides my buddies, my aunt and uncle were there, along with friends from Mappin, Cledir's family, twenty people at most. The atmosphere was great, everybody drinking and laughing, lots of congratulations, happiness to both of you, they said; help me serve, Cledir said, handing me a plate with a slice of cake.

Érica was in the corner of the room, fooling with a dictionary, two dictionaries. She didn't want to dance. In the last few days we'd barely seen each other. I was out of the house all the time and when I got home she'd be asleep, that's how it had to be. Érica didn't want to live in Cledir's house; she said she'd sooner die. After a lot of talk she finally agreed. I won't go till the end of the month, she said. All right, I said. Who's going to pay the rent till then, her? Cledir asked. No, it was Cledir who would pay, but I told Cledir that Érica would pay.

Want some cake? I asked. Hyena, she read, genus Carnivora, the size of a large dog. The hyena, a very ferocious animal that sniffs around tombs to eat cadavers: Manuel Bernardes. Death, like a hyena, opened its ravenous mouth: Guerra Junqueira, Muse on Holiday. I love dictionaries, she said, you learn a lot from dictionaries. My father didn't read books, he read dictionaries. He used to say that if he went to the moon and could only take one thing with him, he'd take a dictionary. Look at this word. I looked: comborço, n. period. What do you think it means? I don't know. Take a guess. A small purse, I said. She laughed. Listen: 1. The lover of a woman in relation to her husband or another lover of the same woman. What could be done, if the dead man arose between them like a ghost, seeing in him a comborço, in her an adulteress, in both, a vile pair?: Veiga Miranda, Fleeing Birds, page 69. Feminine form: comborça. Plural: comborços. Cool, you can keep them, I said. Are they yours? No, they're Cledir's, but she doesn't read, you can keep them. I think the beer's running out, Cledir said, hugging me from behind. Érica closed the dictionary. Those dictionaries were my mother's, Cledir said, she was a teacher. I gave them to Érica, I said. Cledir smiled. She smiled but she didn't like it. You gave them to her? Yes, I didn't think you'd mind. Look, Érica, I'm going to give you a dictionary, I really am, but those belonged to my mother. I kept only a few things of hers, so forgive me, OK? Cledir took the dictionaries from Érica's hand. Go buy some more beer, right now, it's running out.

Érica, look, I'm a real screw-up. Érica didn't even let me finish. She went out in a hurry, following Robinson, and locked herself with Robinson in the bathroom. I asked for the key to Marcão's car and went to the supermarket, bought two more cases of beer, stopped at Cláudio's news-stand. You got a dictionary there? He didn't have a dictionary, but he had an almanac. I bought it; dictionaries and almanacs are the same thing.

When I got back, Érica was at the stereo. She would put on a record, take it off, put on another, take it off, turn up the sound, turn down the sound, scratch the record, turn on the radio and, between times, pop the balloons with a cigarette. She must have been snorting. That no-good Robinson must have given her some coke. Is she crazy, Cledir asked, or is she just trying to irritate me? Nobody can dance, or even talk. It's irritating. Christ, the girl's a royal pain in the ass.

I took Érica to the bedroom, pushed her down on the bed. Now listen, I said, just sit there and listen. I'm not listening to a goddamn thing. I told you I didn't want any coke at this party, I said. Go fly a kite, she huffed, go fly a kite. She started laughing. Fly a kite, how old-fashioned can you get, fly a kite. She was laughing like crazy. Take it, I said. Érica got up from the bed, took the almanac. Did you buy it? Yes. She came up to me and tried to kiss me on the mouth. I didn't let her.

I'll wager you wanted to.

That's stupid.

I'm not stupid and you can screw yourself. And you've wanted to ever since that day. And there's something else: when I went to wish you happiness, I lied. You like me and I want you to screw yourself. I want you to cry in the bathroom, to not be able to go to sleep, for your heart to be as heavy as lead and for you to long for me so much that it cuts you in two. That's what I want, you idiot. And you can stick that almanac up your ass.

She stopped at the door, picked up the almanac. Give it

68

to me, she said, the almanac is mine, and she shoved me in the chest. You asshole, go fuck yourself.

I went back to the living room. Cledir grabbed me to dance. I'm glad Érica left, she's so childish, Cledir said. We danced, making a train and playing at running through the house, the train bumping into things. I remembered Érica's locomotive.

A friend of Cledir's made up a game that went like this. We formed a circle with the bride in the middle. She had to recite a poem, everybody clapping hands, clap, clap, clap, love, love, oh love, clap, clap, clap, Cledir, that's not a poem. I don't know any poems, clap, clap, clap, hands clapping, Cledir pulled me inside the circle, goat-footed, coarse temperaments / raping hamadryad virgins, everybody started laughing, don't try making things up, they said, clap, clap, clap, I didn't make it up, you dummies, that's a poem by a very important man, clap, clap, nobody believed me, we laughed a lot, it was really funny. Robinson stood there laughing in the middle of the circle, without anything to say. Marcão too. We'd been drinking, it was lots of fun. A bunch of fools, my uncle said, do song lyrics count?

That was how my party went. Weddings, engagements, baptisms, anniversaries, I've always found those parties a drag: wakes, funerals, silver-wedding anniversaries, people always doing the same thing, for ten thousand years, getting married, having kids, and going to weddings, funerals, wakes, everything the same. We know what it's like and we go anyway, pointlessly, that stupid chit-chat, deepest sympathy, congratulations, words that mean absolutely nothing, doormat words, so trampled-on, so worn out. That's what I'd always thought, but the truth is that my wedding was fun, it was different, it was enjoyable. It didn't even seem like I was doing the same thing as five hundred million other people, exactly alike; it seemed like my party had been different, the only different wedding of the five hundred million in the world.

At eight pm Cledir and I were alone. Come and see the presents, she said. I was a little bit drunk, at the stage where you've left the ground but aren't yet flying, the stage where you think everything is good: vases are good, hardwood is good, everything's good. Lamp-posts are good, I was at that stage. JOB PROBLEMS PREVENTED ATTENDANCE STOP CONGRATULATIONS STOP AUNT CARMEM. Aunt Carmem is my mother's sister, she said. Look how nice this tea-set is, my girlfriends from Mappin sent it. A piece of crap, I said, so many women, they could have given something more expensive. Seven women and they give a tea-set. Shit, that tea-set is a piece of shit. Peace and joy, a perfect marriage, congratulations from Dr Carvalho and family. I don't understand why Dr Carvalho gave us a freezer, Cledir said. I told you, he likes me. But have you seen what freezers cost? I see them all the time at Mappin, they're real expensive. He's got money, I said. He must have it to burn, then, to give us a freezer, I never saw anything like it.

I pulled Cledir to me, kissed her. Wait, I'm going to get ready, she said.

I stretched out on the bed and waited, and while I waited I turned to the wall the picture frame with the photo of Cledir's parents. A white nightgown. Do you like it? Yes, come here.

Cledir was nervous. I wasn't. I was all right. I lowered the straps, lace, the points of Cledir's breasts were upright, hard. I ran my tongue around them, descended, her thorax, her navel. I opened Cledir's legs, licked, she was dry. I licked, I

70

sucked. It was sweet, very sweet, my wife's juice. I covered her body, stuck my prick inside, cavity, it was hot, of course it was hot, I came.

I came and felt sleepy, very sleepy.

I rolled on my side and went to sleep.

I I

Marriage is just what you think it is: women need to get married and men end up marrying. They need to get married, they need to have children, and men accept the rules because they're tired of the struggle and want peace, that's what marriage is. His name was Humberto and I was looking for a job. I said I was married, a newlywed, and the guy launched into a talk about marriage. I got married, he said, and you know what happened? Take a guess, guess right and you've got the job. I had the impression he was drunk, roaring drunk. C'mon, guess, the job's yours, bridegroom. He was drunk, of course. Speak up, he said, out with it. Something white entered my skull, a stone, a block of granite, I couldn't think of anything. This is an admissions test, bridegroom, don't you want the job? Children, I said, children. He laughed, laughter reeking of alcohol, children, but that wasn't the worst, the worst, he said, is that we're fools. You're a fool, all men are fools, we think: OK, I'll get married and then knock her around a bit, but when the time comes for knocking her around, the best time, in my mind, the time when you break all the bitch's teeth, that's when the man is tied from head to foot, completely tied up, because God, with his dirty tricks, to make sure this shit would go on, didn't teach women to cook or iron, but just one thing: to tie down, understand? He laughed, what a crazy guy, to tie down. I married the devil, he said; I didn't say anything. I married Cledir, my marriage was different. I liked opening the refrigerator door just to look at the apples, the pears, the strawberries, the fruit in the fridge. Every morning I would walk around Cledir's house and say to myself, I'm the husband, she's the wife, we have a bed, and that's our laundry sink, our electric carving knife. I liked it, really liked it, my marriage was enjoyable, hi, love, I clipped an ad from the paper for you, salesman, love, you have sales experience. Listen to this, he said, women need to get married, they need to because they need to have kids, they need to have kids because they need to scream, they need to scream because they don't get pleasure out of any goddamn thing. If they're housewives they think being a housewife is shit; if they work, they're divided. The cows are always dissatisfied: my work, they say, modern life, they say, the mother's role, they say, lovers, frozen food, personal satisfaction, it's difficult to reconcile, they say. A bunch of idiots, what's difficult is making a plane fly. Tramps, damned cows, fat cows. There's that too, they get fat and look like hell. You know why they get fat? They get fat to get everything over with once and for all; basically, women need to destroy the life of at least one man. That's how it is. I think you understand, boy, get married and you're tied down. He laughed loudly, bellowing laughter. His face was red, his nose covered with blackheads. The job's yours, married man, you can come clean up animal shit every day. At night you can go home tired and clean up baby shit, which stinks a lot worse. Once your kid is born, you'll leave here saying that cats and rats shit perfume. He laughed as he said it, leaning his elephant's body against the counter and laughing so much that the counter turned over, feed, birdseed, collars, leashes, cages, rat-traps, everything fell to the floor. I bent over to start picking it up, he was still laughing. Leave it, he said, leave it. It's good for the customers to slip and break a leg. The bridegroom is hired, you can start tomorrow morning, very early. The animals will be shitting all night, waiting for you to show up. I thought of asking about the pay, but I was embarrassed to. See you tomorrow, then, I said, on my way out. He came to the door, go hubby, he shouted, go to your abode, and laughed loudly, go take care of your sweet little wife, and laughed, what a crazy man. People in the street were beginning to look at me, I felt like an idiot. You shitty little hubby, he said, go home sweet home.

I didn't like the owl painted on the door, or the owl's eyes, and inside, that smell of Ajax and manure. My mouth had the taste of copper, and that man laughing, I don't know, I didn't like it. I kept wondering whether it was right for me to take Ezequiel's place, if all this was a sign for me to stay away from there, maybe something trying to punish me. Ezequiel was on the other side now and could work his revenge, Suel too, devils, imps. Men pay for their crimes right here, hell is the earth, hound. I thought about that and stopped in my tracks on the street. I couldn't go anywhere, hound, half man, half goat. I decided to go back to the shop and tell Mr Humberto that I'd had second thoughts and didn't want the job anymore. The devil exists. When I got to the corner, I stopped in my tracks again, went to the bar across the street and ordered Coca-Cola. Mr Humberto was still laughing and screaming and imitating chickens, cock-a-doodle-doo. He was bellowing and flapping his wings, the customers left in horror, and all I had to do was cross the street and say I didn't want the job. I couldn't do it, come clean up the shit, hubby, he said, go say you don't want the job, go ahead, another Coca-Cola, the animals will be shitting all night, waiting for you to show up, go on, go on, man, go take care of your sweet little wife. Go ahead and tell him: Stick this job up your ass. I couldn't do it. I couldn't because I'm ashamed of turning back, I'm ashamed of going forward, I'm ashamed of asking, of receiving, of requesting, losing, I'm ashamed of being poor, of being fucked over, I'm ashamed of not having a pot to piss in. And I'm ashamed of my shoes too. I didn't go. I drank Coca-Cola and thought about my life. Ezequiel was dead, someone would have to sell the animals. Since I first started following Ezequiel I thought about that. I like animals, leaving out cats, those traitors, I like any kind of animal. Selling animals is better than being a hardware representative, salary plus commissions, pizza maker and delivery man, technical salesman, outside salesman, independent salesman, much better.

I bought flowers and went to the Santo Amaro cemetery, I wanted to come to an agreement with Ezequiel. The cemetery was closed. I jumped over the wall and walked down the paths, flowers, so many flowers, flowers are like cows, they accept the world. Priests, pastors, voodoo priests, they all say the same thing: accept everything, accept the darkness, accept the money, the knife wounds and the happiness, accept. Look at the pasture and learn from the cows, accept, learn from the flowers, they say, accept, and men accept everything, anything, especially the darkness, but they learn nothing, that's the problem, that's the difference. Men can't learn to learn.

Ezequiel, my friend, I've come to make a deal with you: starting today, every month I'll give part of my pay to your mother, and you can rest easy that she won't suffer any deprivation as long as I live. I'll look after your mother like she was my own. But you have to promise to leave me in peace. Each of us will live in our own world and take care of our own work. I killed you, Ezequiel, but not out of malice, I even thought you were a cool guy. I killed you because the world's a lousy place and the evil in the world crushes a man's heart. That's what happened with me.

I left the cemetery feeling calm. I was going home, Cledir should already have got there from Mappin, it was eight-thirty in the evening, she'd be happy to learn that I'd found a job. She'd fix some beans and I'd talk about the new job. Great, she'd say, now we can start saving, we can open a savings account, we can buy things, a car, a motorcycle, a microwave, shaving cream, lots of things. I'm going to give you a present, Cledir, a red dress, sandals, a wig, a Roberto Carlos record. I was heading home, dying to tell Cledir the news, a necklace, earrings, but suddenly I missed Gorby, the pig; I needed his company, so I decided to go by Érica's to get him. Cledir wouldn't mind, I hadn't discussed the subject with her yet, but I had a job, she couldn't say anything. I was going to come home with a job and my pig. Lots of news, she would say. She'd like it, Cledir was real cool, I told myself, how great that I married Cledir.

Érica was in the bathroom. I went straight to the backyard, Gorby was sleeping. I scooped him up in my arms and sat by the kitchen door. You've grown, you rascal.

I hadn't seen Érica since the wedding, I hadn't even thought about her. I was a married man, I had a job, the sound of the shower tormented me, shhhhhhhhhhhhhh, the water, the shower, I felt like seeing Érica take a bath, seeing her without any clothes on. I went into the bathroom, hi,

Erica. Get out of here, you idiot. I stood there, she covered her breasts with her arms, get out of here or I'll scream. I couldn't move, her navel, her legs, her feet, get out, she screamed, get out of here, her wet hair, get out of here. I got out, I got out and went to look for a ladder in the yard, I don't know why I did that, I got a ladder and spied on her. I could watch her from the hallway, she was still taking a shower, her ass, a marvelous ass, I opened my fly and took out my cock and closed my eyes and thought that man is strong, man struggles, man wins, man conquers, man creates, man builds, and suddenly, plop, Érica yanked on the ladder, son of a bitch, I fell, my legs hurt, Érica threw the ladder on top of me. You idiot, so you think that's how it is? Is that what it is, you want to fuck? I came to fetch Gorby, I said. Liar, you came here to fuck because that's all you think about day and night, you went and married that bore Cledir. Cledir isn't a bore, I said. She's a bore all right. My leg really hurt, help me up, I said. You came here because you're crazy to fuck me, it's good to want something. You can roll on the floor from wanting it so much, see what it's like to want something, dying for something. You want it? You broke my leg, I said, I can't move. Érica sat on my stomach, you idiot, I've been waiting here for you, waiting for a long time, she said, and kissed me. My leg stopped hurting. Érica entered me, each of us entered the other, in the darkest and brightest parts that existed inside us. Érica drew me into something warm, something very warm and very powerful, I love you, she said, I smile, I drink, I smoke, I dance, I snort, I laugh, I lie, I spit, I sing, but inside I'm always sad because you killed Suel, because you married Cledir, you only fuck me, you're my enemy, you're my enemy and I love you, that's not right, you make me suffer. Érica rested against my shoulder and I liked her being weak and me being strong, woman and man; we slept.

I woke up at three am. I have to go, Érica, Cledir must be worried. Érica punched me in the chest, that makes me so mad, she said, so mad, you married that bore, you're going to leave that bore, aren't you? I have to go. I tried kissing Érica, she pushed me away, then grabbed me and kissed me. Don't think I'm silly, OK? I'm not silly, I have a silly face but I'm a very intelligent woman, understand? Very intelligent and very experienced. I found that funny, intelligent and experienced, shit. Érica, let me go. She laughed too, you can go, it's true, you're going to get fucked with me. You think it's bad for me to take Gorby? No, she said, but you mustn't forget to bathe him. I'll bathe him, I said. And feed him bananas too, he loves bananas. I'll give him bananas, don't worry.

When I got home, Cledir was asleep. I put Gorby in the yard and came to bed. Hi, she said, smiling, that's right, smiling, you were out a long time, what time is it? One o'clock, I said, the liar said it was one o'clock, it was four. Where were you, dear? Just like that: dear, in a sweet tone. I went to fetch Gorby, I said. Cledir hugged me, I was worried, you should have let me know, love. I was worried. I got into bed, turned my back, I didn't want Cledir to see the face of a scoundrel. She intertwined our legs, our arms, it's so good to sleep holding each other, isn't it, Máiquel? Tying down.

12

Robinson is funny, every morning he wakes up, goes to the mirror, and says: Hey, man, this is your day, you're a lucky guy, everything's great, everything's going to work out fine. I'm different, when I wake up I say right away: Hey, dog, stick your head under the pillow because today's going to be shit and tomorrow's going to be the same shit. I don't feel like getting out of bed. Or opening the window. I don't feel like going to work. Eating ice cream. Seeing people. All I want to do is smoke. I didn't want to be that way. I wanted to be like those guys who drive around with bumper stickers on their cars. I believe in elves, Donald Duck smiling, Daisy smiling, Disneyland, I Love New York, I Love Ribeirão Preto, those guys you see at the entrances to barbecue restaurants. But I'm not that way, if I wear a yellow shirt it doesn't work, it's ugly, it doesn't go with anything. I don't go with yellow, with red; I'm a gray man. I read all that stuff in the paper, Iraq moves troops, refugees flee Burundi for Zaire, none of that happens to me. I wasn't in the attack that killed twenty-two people in Tel Aviv. I didn't see the Vietnam war, I wasn't exterminated by police death squads in Rio de Janeiro, but when I see those news items on television I say: I know that shit, I know what the blood of those kids is like who appear in the arms of volunteer nurses in Rwanda, I know what they feel. I know the pain. They want to escape the Hutu attacks, says the anchorman. I also try to run away. I don't want to get out of bed. I don't want to leave the house. I don't want to go to work. I'm afraid of dying. I once told Érica that when I laugh I have the impression that my face is cracking, breaking, that my face is made of ceramic. She was studying English; she put down the book and kissed me, we kissed for a long time, and suddenly I felt in my mouth the taste of her tears. I opened my eyes, Érica's face was covered with tears. It pierced my heart and I began to cry too, just like her, silently, the two of us crying, and that's how it was, we fucked crying.

It's good to tell these stories, it's a way of remembering that before becoming a dog I was something else, I was a man, I was good. Fair. I was honest, pure, I was a casserole that kept warm all the things they threw at me to cook. On my birthday I awoke without the strength to do anything. I thought about skipping work, thought about dumping Cledir, thought about running away from São Paulo, but I didn't do any of those things. I got up and said: Hey, man, today's your birthday, you have to do like Robinson, you're a lucky guy, everything's great, everything's going to work out fine. You're not going to dump anything. You're not going to destroy anything. You're going to go on. You're going to make your bundle. Cook. Create. I went to the bathroom and stood there in front of the mirror, dancing like those black guys and making up a rap song: Today's my birthday/I'm happy as a clam/Gettin' lots of presents/And I don't give a damn/I'm gonna make it big/I'm gonna end up rich/Anyone says different's/A crazy sonofbitch/Gonna wear Brooks Brothers/And only fancy shoes/Live in ritzy mansions/And never sing the blues/I'm a dentist, a lawyer, an exec, a tycoon/Today's my day to make it, I'm shooting for the moon.

That's what I did, I took a shower and left for work, full of goodwill. Life's like that: you have to make an effort. If the work is lousy, you force yourself to like it; if the pay is low, never mind, put your nose to the grindstone. Your wife's going to have a baby, OK, so that's how it goes, women have babies. If you're fucked over, it doesn't matter, go on turning nuts, tightening screws, chew gum, do everything right and relax on Sundays. My effort didn't bring any results, I spent an absolutely normal day cleaning up hamster shit; the only good thing that happened was seeing Mr Humberto's wife give him a slap in the face. You fool, she said, and wham. Take it easy, Maria, he said with tears in his voice, take it easy my ass, and wham. I love watching slapping scenes.

I went home and found Cledir in the kitchen, standing over the pans. She gave me a pair of navy-blue shoes as a birthday present. Go take a bath, I'm making a surprise for you, she said.

I bathed, shaved, put on my favorite clothes, a black shirt and jeans. The shoes were really pretty. Happy birthday. I looked in the mirror, twenty-three years old, my arms were strong. I went back to the living room, Cledir was having a lively conversation with a guy and a girl I'd never seen before. Hi, she said, this is Marcia who works with me and this is her boyfriend Rodomildo. Happy birthday, they said, you two go ahead and talk, come with me, Marcia. The two women left, I turned on the television, the president of the US announced that American troops were beginning a peaceful occupation. I sell insurance, Rodomildo said, but I haven't sold anything, you'd think we were living in Switzerland. Nobody wants to buy insurance against auto theft. I changed the channel: Corinthians and Santos with a shot at the play-offs, a real disgrace that Sport beat Corinthians two to nothing, a disgrace, a real disgrace. I changed the channel, I didn't want to talk to him. Cledir told me you're a salesman; I kept quiet, that's always my tactic for getting people not to talk to me, just stare into space and pretend I'm deaf, and usually it works. Come on in, Cledir said, we went, the table was set, plates, beer, and in the middle an enormous pig with potatoes and broccoli. Umm, it smells wonderful, Rodomildo said. My heart was racing. No, no, it can't be, I thought. I opened the kitchen door and Gorby wasn't there, where's Gorby? What a question, love. Cledir smiled, embarrassed, and it was only then that I saw she had a twisted mouth like her mother, roast pig to celebrate your birthday. She smiled. I was paralyzed. Murderer, you murdering cow. I felt like grabbing the potatoes and the broccoli and shoving it all down her throat and in her ears. Sit down, Máiquel, what's gotten into you? Umm, it really does smell good. Cledir started slicing Gorby. He was treated with kid gloves, she said, we've been fattening this pig since our engagement, she said. How could Cledir have the courage? I thought about slaughtering him at Christmas, Cledir continued, but it's still a long time till Christmas, and it's better to have turkey at Christmas, besides which, the pig in the yard, you can't imagine the work. I felt like smashing Cledir's face, you tramp, don't you have a heart? She cut off the left leg of my friend Gorby and served it to me, served Rodomildo, who loves pork, loves every kind of meat, served Marcia. They started eating and I felt like crying. Gorby, Gorby's little eyes. Aren't you going to eat, Máiquel? I was like a zombie at that table. Cledir was happy, quickly eating my pig and talking loudly to her Mappin friends, Máiquel's salary is a joke, and they ate my pig, I make more than he does, the knife, I pay for running the house, the knife, the others were also eating fast, bunch of ravenous pigs, cutting, the pay's good at Mappin, she said, the knife, stab with the fork, but it's hard to make ends meet by myself, Cledir said, the house, the knife, chewing, the house belonged to my mother, swallowing, we moved in, forkful, we moved in with everything furnished, just imagine if we had to pay rent. Of course Máiquel's salary helps, eating my pig, my very own pig, and badmouthing me and my work, humiliating me, and want some more, dear? I bought him a pair of shoes, show them the shoes, love, aren't they pretty?

I was so angry that I got up and went to the bedroom, Cledir behind me. What was it, Máiquel, why didn't you finish eating? Take these shoes, I said, throwing them in her face. I want my old shoes back. I don't need you to buy shoes for me. I turned the closet upside down, looked under the bed, where are my shoes? I threw them out, she said. You threw out my shoes? Yes. You did that? You threw out my only pair of shoes? Love, the shoes had holes in them. How dare you throw out my shoes? Máiquel, for heaven's sake, what's got into you? Why are you so mad?

I left there barefoot and started walking. It was raining. I didn't want to have anything to do with her, the murdering whore. I kept walking and feeling rage, rat, hate, I screamed, rat, I screamed as loud as I could, I walked, it was raining, my heart heavy, oil, petroleum, I walked, not knowing where I was going, when I saw I was in front of Dr Carvalho's house. I sat in the gutter, stayed there, lots of rain. Suddenly, headlights in my eyes, Gabriela stuck her head out of the automobile, hi, she said, what are you doing there? Rat. She got out of the car: What? You're all wet, let's go inside. Where are your shoes? She took me inside, gave me a towel, you're trembling, wait while I call my father. The television on, most profitable stocks, the sale of shares fluctuates greatly, investors are chasing dollars in the parallel market, the Central Bank has lowered surcharge rates. Dr Carvalho came in holding a glass of whiskey, Máiquel, did something happen? Gabriela, fetch a T-shirt for him, and some sneakers. I'll fetch you a drink, there's something the matter with you. He left to fetch the drink, Gabriela came in with the T-shirt, let me help you, she took off my shirt and ran her hand over my chest, you're strong, she said. I wasn't strong. I put on the sneakers, Dr Carvalho returned with the whiskey, told Gabriela to leave us by ourselves, you need something to pick you up, son, drink this. I drank, the whiskey was good, it warmed me as it went down. Life seemed a little better. Have you given anymore thought to Sílvio's offer? I nodded, before remembering that Sílvio was the man I'd met at the dinner at Dr Carvalho's house, the man who recycled garbage and wanted me to kill someone. The television was showing ads for food, pussy, blankets, shoes, houses, automobiles, watches, teeth, high school, girlfriends, stereos, respect, baloney sandwiches, ice cream, soccer balls, cough syrup, socks, movies, filet mignon. That's the spirit, my boy. You did the right thing. Let's go to my office. We're going to have a talk about that son of a bitch who's making Sílvio's life unbearable.

I3

A labama has it, Alaska doesn't. Arizona, Arkansas, California, Colorado, Florida. The District of Columbia may adopt the death penalty, said the headline from three years ago. The Senate has already approved the bill. All that's left is the House. In Japan there's also a death penalty. I was reading the material that Dr Carvalho gave me, Missouri yes, Nebraska yes, Oklahoma yes, North Dakota no. States, democratic First World countries. I read the stories, drank vodka, the revolver in my belt. I crumpled up the newspaper, crossed the street, the lights in the shack were already out. I knocked and seconds later a woman came to the door. Is Neno in? He's asleep, she said. I need to talk to him, it's important. A young boy came to the door and stood there looking at me. Go call your father, I said. I don't have a father. I want to speak to Neno. I'm Neno. They wanted me to kill this kid? Thin legs, the face of somebody who'd been hungry all his life, twelve years old at most, they wanted me to kill a twelve-year-old boy? No fucking way. My mistake, I told the kid. I turned my back and walked off, kill a twelve-year-old boy, what are they thinking of? Begging Dr Carvalho's pardon, I'd kill a grown man, I'd kill an old man, I'd kill blacks, poor people, society women, Japanese, I'd kill anybody, but I wouldn't kill children. Or a pregnant woman. That I wouldn't do, because if I cut my flesh, what would come out was blood not shit. I was going to say that to Dr Carvalho, maybe he didn't know it. I walked on, my pocket full of money I'd have to return. Fuck it, they're not making a patsy out of me.

14

Tables with white tablecloths. Couples. A small stage, a man singing if you believe my heart is made of paper, you're wrong, for it's not. They're looking at us, all the people are looking at us, I look like a dog. Fuck it, I don't care, I've got money, money that Dr Carvalho gave me.

Steak with chips	$14.00
Steak with onions	$16.00
Steak with egg	$19.00
Steak house style	$20.00

Order whatever you like, Érica, I've got the money.

I don't want to eat, I want to drink. Order whiskey, she said. Order that one there, the expensive one. Good drink is expensive drink.

I had just told Érica what had happened, the boy I didn't kill. Look, Máiquel, I'm going to tell you something I read in the almanac, that almanac you gave me. You know I like to study, I like to find out things. I'm learning to speak

English: My name is Érica, I speak English. You need to learn English. You need to travel and see the things that I saw with my father. You need to stop selling birdseed, because selling birdseed won't get you anywhere. If you saw the alligators in the Wetlands, if you saw ten miles of deserted beach, the golden sand, really gold, like gold itself, there in Bahia, near Cabrália, you'd see all this is shit. They want you to kill a boy of twelve? Shit, let's bail, haven't you got the money? Let's bail with the guy's money. The money will run out. So what if it does? Suel always used to say, money'll turn up. And it does turn up. Then we spend it. And some more turns up. You already killed Suel, you killed Ezequiel. That's going to drop you in deep shit, and soon. Listen: before long you'll be arrested. You'll be tried and convicted. You'll get thirty years in prison.

Tell me what you read in the almanac, I said.

I'll tell you. I'll tell you because it's what's happening with you.

Érica was a very intelligent girl, and more and more I liked being with her. Keen eyes, muscles, very different from Cledir. Érica loved to drink and dance. She liked to laugh. And Cledir waiting on me for supper. Growing my child in her belly, cooking, a pure thing, sincere, sure. Érica was not to be trusted and would cheat on me. She was going to cheat on me, I could sense it in every word coming from her mouth. The way she looked at the waiter, at the young guy at the next table, the way she tossed back her hair when we fucked on the sofa. Signs of cheating. Cledir would never cheat on me. But the problem is that there's no such thing as intuition in love. In love, there are only steps, those steps you climb, climb, all you want to do is climb, and I was climbing.

Do you know what a kamikaze is?

That was Érica's way of dominating me, the almanacs she read, the newspapers, the television reports, the travel, the dictionaries, the correspondence courses in English, the things she knew, sang, recited. I always felt ignorant beside Érica, and that held me back, tied me down, left me plugged into Érica's outlet. Kami means divine and kaze means wind. Divine wind, that almanac you gave me is a real pisser. The typhoons that wiped out the two Mongol fleets had that name, kamikaze. The Mongol Kublai Khan would have swallowed up Japan except for those typhoons, understand? So in the Second World War the Japanese, who didn't know what to do against the American troops who were advancing at full speed, came up with the kamikazes. Only the kamikazes could do anything about those guys, the Americans. So they invented suicide pilots, a crazy thing, guys who got in their planes and blew up the enemy, died along with the enemy. That's what's happening to you. They want you to blow up the enemy, except that you're going to have to blow up with them, that's the heart of the matter.

I'll never forget what Érica told me. I laughed out loud like she'd said something really dumb, I laughed because I didn't understand anything, laughed at my own stupidity. Today I know what a kamikaze is. Those guys made me into a kamikaze, an ignorant kamikaze who didn't know the plane was going to explode. Today I can tell who the sons of bitches are, the inventors of the suicide pilots, just by looking at their shoes I can spot a son of a bitch. Sons of bitches like moccasins, they like tassels, they like little gold chains on their instep, their shoes are wine-colored. If you see a guy with shoes that color, get out of there because at the first opportunity he's going to fuck you. But back then I didn't know anything. Dr Carvalho took care of my rotten teeth, I thought. Dr Carvalho invited me to dinner at his house. Dr Carvalho introduced me to his friend the industrialist. That's what I thought about. They gave me whiskey, they gave me tropical pineapple, they made me feel like a wet dog, they made me feel ashamed of my shitty shoes, so I thought, shit, these guys are really cool. I'm a shitass and they're cool, lower your eyes because they're really cool. They've got the house that I don't have, the family I don't have, the car I don't have, these guys are cool. They humiliated me and I said, you're cool. They made me ashamed of being who I was, of coming from where I came from, of having what I had, and I said, you're cool. They had no respect for me. They put me down, and I thought it was right, I thought it was correct. That's how it was.

I love my dog, Érica said, in English. Yesterday I saw a woman with a sticker on her car, I love my dog. Know what I did? I picked up some dog shit that was on the sidewalk and put it on the windshield of the woman's car. It's people like that I'm talking about, she said. People like that. Their kind makes me sick. They love their dogs, love their poodles, love their Dalmatians, their five-hundred-dollar German shepherds, they train their dogs, they teach their dogs to shit on the sidewalk for us to step on the shit and remember their stinking dogs, to be afraid of their ferocious dogs, they teach them everything. Dogs learn fast. If you slip up, you'll learn, Máiquel. You'll learn. You'll learn to bark. To attack. To bite. To sniff out cocaine. To eat table scraps. That's the way it is, you learn, it's easy to learn to hate. It's easier to learn to hate than to cook or to use a computer. They say, that's shit, you believe it, that's shit. It stinks. It really stinks, I can smell the stench. It's rotten. Rotten, it's rotten, we learn. Man learns everything. That's why man progresses. Science progresses. The United States progresses. Industry. Technology. But the human heart, I heard a man say this on television, a very important man, the human heart doesn't progress. So, Érica said, progress does no fucking good, vaccines to save dummies, that's the truth. But that's beside the point. What matters is that you have to be careful with those guys because otherwise, otherwise you're going to learn what they want to teach you. You're going to get fucked.

I was in that restaurant, drinking whiskey with Érica, with Dr Carvalho's money. I didn't know any of that, and I didn't try to understand any of it. I was fed up with the subject. I didn't want to talk about it. I was an idiot, I laughed and changed the subject. Let's get out of here, I told Érica.

We went to Gonzaga's bar, ran into some friends, and did all those things, smoke and snort and listen to music. Robinson was happy because he was going to spend the weekend in Rio de Janeiro, a job he bagged. Go see the Christ statue. Go see the Tijuca forest. Go see Copacabana Beach. And if you find a girlfriend, take her to sleep at the Tifany. Ask for a front room and show her the boats. Show her the lovers who come to the Tifany. Show her the hundred-year-old trees in Paris Square. See the pigeons in Paris Square. Érica was always saying interesting things and that turned me on, really made me want to fuck, to swallow Érica whole, to plant my flag in that territory. Let's go, I said in her ear. We went to her house, to my old house, as soon as we got into the kitchen she jumped onto the table, a carnivore, her legs wrapped around me, ravenous, bite my mouth, she said. I bit, I entered, I traversed, and when I was crossing over, I felt my heart floating, inside of Érica I was like that, a good man, free of pain.

I went home thinking about the lie I'd have to tell Cledir, thinking also that I should get rid of Érica. Every day I thought that, and every day I went back to Érica. I went back to Érica and to Cledir. I fucked Érica and I fucked Cledir. It was good with Érica, it was good with Cledir. I lied to Érica, said I didn't fuck Cledir. And I lied to Cledir too. It's easy to lie, you have to look the person in the eye and tell them what they want to hear. Are you doing anything with Érica? Of course not. Are you screwing that bore? Obviously not. I had spent all of Dr Carvalho's money and would have to make up some lie for him too. Distribute lies. I was going to say that Neno, the little thief, had run off to Mato Grosso. It was a good idea. Except I had to speak with Neno first: Man, get the hell away from here, they're going to kill you. I was going to do all that, the very next day. First I had to sleep.

The lights were on at my house, strange. Cledir didn't usually wait for me in the living room. As I approached the gate I heard a cry, Aunt Rosa sobbing. She hugged me. She shook me. And said she wanted to die. Robinson's been killed, she said. Ta ta ta ta ta ta, that's the sound of a machine gun. They yanked him out of bed, she said. They took him out to the street. They made him get down on his knees. They machine gunned Robinson. Ta ta ta ta ta ta, bursts of thirty-two shots. Do something, she said, they killed Robinson.

Robinson teaching me to swim. Robinson at the stadium, picking on the Palmeiras fans. Robinson dancing rap. Robinson smoking grass and saying he believed in God, that God loved him, he felt that, God was a cool guy. God is a scream in the middle of the street, Érica read that someplace. A scream in the middle of the street. I wanted to say that to Robinson when I saw his body riddled with holes in the middle of the street.

I knew that Robinson had died by mistake. Selective killings. Messages. Like in Bolivia. Colombia. Venezuela. I was the target. They wanted to kill me because I killed Suel. The wager. My blond hair. Suel turned his back on me and jived off down the street, holding hands with his girl. Go ahead and shoot, he said, kill me from behind. I shot the first round. Suel hit the ground, he must have died instantly. Now they want to kill me. They're going to kill me, I killed Ezequiel. I'm going to tell you something, son. You have lousy teeth. I'm a dentist. I have a problem and you have lousy teeth. We can help one another. You help me, I'll help you. I'll fix your teeth for free and you'll do something for me. Agreed? Ezequiel turned around and saw me. I pulled out the gun, took aim, and bang. I missed with the first shot. Bang. I missed a second time. The third one caught him in the thigh, the fourth one in the chest. He fell, I missed with two more shots, Ezequiel was still alive, I yanked a piece of wood from a fence around a tree and threw myself on him. I hit him in the head, hammered at him, hammered, put out his eyes, I rammed the wooden spike into the rapist's heart, I'd seen this on television, Ezequiel vomited blood and died. I killed Suel. I killed Ezequiel because I killed Suel. They killed Robinson because I killed Suel. Now they were going to kill me.

The sky was full of clouds, there was lead in the sky. My family stood around the corpse, crying, the coffin, the tomb, and the priest. Not me. I got my revolver and left, hatred growing inside me. I walked and walked, till I came to where I was going. House number 7 had the window open. I knocked on the door. Neno, the boy Sílvio wanted me to kill, appeared. He appeared and didn't give me time to

93

do anything, he jumped over the wall, jumped over fences, turning right and left, with me behind him. Neno went into a bar and hid behind the counter. Everybody on the floor, I said. I drew closer, in firing position. Neno was crouched beside some Coca-Cola bottles, praying. Residents set fire to bus. Drug dealers adopt lighter rifles. Businessman found dead in car trunk. Sixteen cars stolen at Rio club. Firearms for personal defense, three easy payments. Police invade hillside slum, killing three. All I could see was the blood on his face, says his mother. A good day for the police, says the newscaster. Animated cartoon, a smiling man shooting an old man. Operation was legal, says administration. The problem, says Dr Carvalho, the problem with those kids is that the police catch them and the courts let them go. Neno begged me in the name of God not to kill him. But I didn't believe in God anymore. I believed in ulcers. I'm going to kill you, you son of a bitch. I'm going to kill you because, starting today, I'm the killer. I'm the bars, the dog, the wall, the broken glass. I'm the barbed wire, the steel door. I'm the killer. Bang. Bang. Bang.

15

Bang. Bang. Bang. I hit with all three shots, three tomato-sauce cans went flying, somersaulting and falling on top of the garbage. I went to the wall, placed five bottles, I preferred bottles, the pieces of glass shattering, I liked the sound.

Until you kill the first guy you think there's this business of learning to kill. Learning to kill is like learning to die; one day you die and that's it. Nobody learns to kill. That's bullshit from cops. Everybody is born knowing how. If you have a gun in your hand, that's all there is to it; you already know everything you need to know. It's like the first time you fuck; you think you don't know how, but your body does everything by itself, something inside does it for you. It's the same thing.

Anyway, I trained every day, it could be raining or sweltering, at lunchtime I would stop selling birdseed and go to a vacant lot near my house, snort a few lines, and start shooting. It was frustrating at first, and I felt like giving up, I couldn't hit even the large targets. One day, Érica drew a heart on a banana tree, listen, man, you've got to think this is the only thing there is, forget everything else, aim here, only here, you need to learn to concentrate, forget that I'm wearing a short blouse. Stop looking at my legs. Do you want to be a slave to your brain or your hormones? Brain. Bang, I hit it. Brain, bang, hit it. Brain, bang, bang, hit it, hit it. Heart, this is my heart, she said in English, bang, very good, brain. Érica brought me luck, from that day on I started training with that heart, with my brain. When the banana tree was dying, I had her draw another heart on another banana tree. I improved a lot. You're getting good at this, she said. And I was. I was changing, weapons change everything. In the old days, when I went out I would just look at my own feet. I didn't see the street, the people, the sun, the news-stands, the ads. I only saw my own shitty shoes, I saw dog shit, I saw cigarette butts, paper, bottle caps, trash. I learned to walk once I started using weapons. To crush sidewalks. I learned to look ahead of me, at people's insides, their neurons, their livers. I changed. I was no longer the same man as before, I was a killer. Today I know that you can turn into a piece of shit, a rat, a mangy dog, and even then you're trying to give a certain look of dignity to it all, trying to see it all as something natural. Killing people, OK, we kill, war, people struggle, it's good, it's bad, it doesn't much matter. I didn't want to know about anything, I just wanted to do what I did right, that's what I wanted.

The bullets ran out. Érica applauded. She was sitting on the hood of an abandoned car, smoking, wearing very high platform shoes. Fingernails painted red. Very good, she said, now come here, let's fuck. She always said that, in the most unexpected situations, when I was working, at home, washing the dishes for Cledir, at the bar, talking with my buddies, she would put her mouth to my ear, time to fuck. I enjoyed obeying. I took the cigarette out of her mouth, she stuck her tongue into mine, took out my gum and stuck it on the roof of the car. We fucked.

Black pants, black shirt, black belt. I crossed my arms in front of the mirror, I felt good in those clothes. The boots, Érica called to the salesgirl, please, dear, look for a size 39 pair of boots in the footwear section. Black. It was a uniform. It had the elegance of a uniform, besides which it was black, at night no one would see. And blood, blood stands out less on black. I tried on the boots. Érica took off her dark glasses and put them on my face. Perfect, she said, that's the thing. We'll take it.

We also bought ropes, a flask, a penknife, and other small items.

I should have stopped by the pet shop. Mr Humberto flew into a rage whenever I didn't show up, but it was very nice being with Érica. We played a game like this: I would see a guy wearing a rug and say to her, I'll pay you five bucks if you'll pull off that guy's toupee. I'll pay five for you to kiss that woman on the back of the neck, kiss her and say, sorry, it was an accident. We had a load of laughs about it, it was lots of fun. We walked slowly, playing around, sometimes I would kiss Érica, imitating her way of speaking, motherrr fuckerrr, rrreal rrrotten, and she'd pull me off the sidewalk, you idiot, there's nothing worse than the way you people from São Paulo talk, you don't even pronounce your s's, you cretin.

We bought ice cream. Érica wanted to go to the eight o'clock show to see Karate Kid 4. I love the Karate Kid, did you see Karate Kid 2, the moment of truth continues? You have to see it. We were like that, laughing, in love, when

Cledir got off the bus. I'm sure she saw us holding hands. She was carrying some packages. You're enormous, Érica said, how many pounds have you put on? Cledir smoothed her hair, she always did that when she felt uneasy. I was immensely sad, that immense belly, all those packages, let me give you a hand, I said. Aren't you going there anymore? Érica asked. Where are you two going? No, I said, I'm going home. Érica. Bye.

We walked away, when I got to the corner, Érica called me. I ran to her, my ice cream fell on the ground. I'll pay you five bucks for you to tell her from right here: Cledir, we're going to the movies. We laughed. Can't be, I said. Asshole. Goddamn asshole, it's all over, she said. Don't show your face around me, you idiot.

Érica turned her back and left, without swaying her hips.

16

The plan was simple: I had to go to the dance and get the guy, Conan. I wasn't working alone. Besides Marcão, Zé Galinha and Enoque were part of the group. Zé was called that because he used to steal chickens when he first started out, and Enoque had that biblical name because of his mother and father, who were very religious.

I'd never been to a funk dance, I had no idea they were so much fun. The dance is simple: you have to punch whoever's in front of you and then cross the room, gangs are formed, you join one of them, that's the move, hitting the others. People say they go there because they like to dance, because they like the music, because they're black, because they're white, because funk is culture. I don't believe any of that; they go there to punch people, that's the truth of it.

Conan was already drunk, but I refilled his glass. I had struck up a conversation with him and he already considered me his friend, spending my time, my money, asked if I wanted a woman, you're cool, I said. He disappeared into the middle of the crowd and returned in a couple of minutes with two girls. I didn't even look at their faces, I wanted to dance. We danced, the four of us, I threw a guy on the floor, kicked him in the stomach, kicked him in the mouth, I remembered my father, I was three years old, kick, the two of us returning home, with me in one arm, the chicken in the other, the butcher behind, kick, you didn't pay for the chicken, the butcher said, my father was outraged at the accusation and, whap, hit the man in the chest with the chicken, the live chicken, whap, the guy ran and, whap, covered with blood, whap, my father killed the chicken on the butcher's back, funk, the guy on the ground, kick, Conan grabbed me, funk, shook me, you trying to kill the guy? You looking to get thrown out of here?

I asked Conan if the girls wanted to go somewhere, it'll be cool, I said. Do you two like marijuana? It was a mistake, they did.

The gunmetal-brown Dodge Dart was parked at the curb. We got in. I started the car and before I could signal, they appeared in the middle of the street, three of them, side by side, drinking cans of Coca-Cola, boots, belts, weapons visible. Marcão stuck the revolver in Conan's face; out, he told the girls. They jumped out. Enoque got in the front seat, Marcão and Zé Galinha in the back, with Conan squeezed between them. He was scared shitless and saying the same blah-blah-blah as always.

I put on a tape real loud and took the highway. Vodka, I felt good, driving a fast car was something that gave me a good feeling, just like TV commercials, a car speeding over a dirt road, the woman at the wheel is drop-dead gorgeous, blue eyes, country house, the man, his black horse, muscles. He gallops to the gate of the ranch, the blue-eyed woman arrives, the man on horseback, her in the car, they go on, happy, get out in front of the mansion, they kiss. The car of the year, says the announcer. I think about the couple. After they go into the house, what are they going to do? They're going to fuck, that's what everybody thinks. Until I met their type, that's what I thought too. Dentists, businessmen, lawyers, industrialists, civil servants, doctors and executives; guys like that don't like to fuck. Especially the young ones. First they have to buy a CD player, a computer, sign contracts, buy a brand-new car, have kids, impress the neighbors, screw up their marriage, wash the car, mistreat the maid, if there's any time left, they fuck. I drove along the highway, thinking about the horse, the money, me fucking that blonde. I remembered Ezequiel, the rapist, he smiled at me, I didn't like it. I lit a joint and we smoked and in the early morning the record player spinning a song, playing B B King endlessly, I said to Marcão that I thought the lyrics went: changing a bikini over and over. Marcão had a laughing fit, we both laughed like shit. I imagined Tim Maia, I think it was Tim Maia, I was shit-faced, listening to a song, loose as a goose on the sofa, with that Santa Claus belly of his, and his wife changing her bikini over and over, you know, those artists are really nuts, they do things like that, I said, they have liposuction and die, they break their girlfriend's arm, they eat pineapples for a week to lose five pounds, that's the kind of thing, they do that, they climb on top of tables in restaurants. And they change bikinis over and over, Marcão added, and we laughed even harder.

At the end of Guarapiranga Avenue I turned right and parked the car by a ravine, told my men to wait. Marcão and I rolled another joint. We smoked, there was a moon in the sky, stars, we smoked stretched out on the ground. I miss Robinson, Marcão said. Me too. He said that with him it was different, I want to tell you something about Robinson, something you don't know, a thing between him and me, he said. Him and me, he said. The problem with marijuana, with alcohol, with drugs in general, is that they unlock doors, people right away start wanting to dump their garbage on whoever's with them, sexual garbage, professional garbage, domestic garbage, I don't want to hear it, I said. Garbage. I got up. Between him and me. Marcão followed me.

In the distance, I saw the scene. The prisoner's hands and feet were tied, his pants around his ankles. I'm going to give you a plate of shit, Zé Galinha said, if you eat it, you go free. It wasn't the first time Zé Galinha had dreamed up such things. I walked faster. Enoque was holding the plate with the sack of shit, it's all here, he told Zé Galinha.

I quickly untied Conan's hands. What's the deal, Máiquel, let me finish my work. He's going to eat shit with a spoon, Máiquel, and you're going to let me do it.

Nobody's eating shit, I said. Put your clothes on, I told Conan. Conan was trembling so much he couldn't even get his pants on. I helped him, fastened his belt. Zé Galinha wouldn't stop talking, goddamn right he's going to eat shit, Zé Galinha said, he's going to, he's going to do it, I didn't set up this circus for nothing, I didn't shit in that plastic bag for fun, that son of a bitch is going to eat shit, yessir, he sure as hell is. I grabbed the plate out of Zé Galinha's hands and threw it as far as I could, what's wrong, Máiquel? Just look, you got shit on my shoes, he said, you got my pants dirty with shit, man. What's the matter, you feel bad for Conan? Is that what it is? I've had it up to here with you, man, what're you thinking, who you think you are, man? You're a piece of shit, that's what you are. A piece of shit, he said. I took out the gun and fired, hit him in the head. Zé Galinha fell dead.

Marcão and Enoque avoided looking at me.

Conan was trembling, thank you, he said. Conan also avoided looking me in the eye. He was looking at my shoes, as if God were there, my shoe with its little gold chain. I shot Conan three times in the head.

My Baby, that's what it said on the cover. I don't want any my baby, my first steps, nothing like that, I want a simple album, no gold letters, no doodads. The salesgirl looked through the shelves a bit more and handed me one with a blue cover, my memories, this one is simpler. It wasn't perfect but I bought it anyway.

I went home, Cledir wasn't back from Mappin yet, I opened the kitchen cupboard, took out some alcohol. Removed the drawings of flowers on the sides and clipped the news item. Youth executed in Guarapiranga.

The body of Pedro dos Santos, who went by the nickname Conan, was discovered by a resident of the area on a narrow dirt road known as Itupu, on the south side of the city. I was going to work, the resident said, and thought it was a drunk sleeping it off. It wasn't till I got close to him that I saw he was dead as a doornail.

I pasted the clipping in the new album and wrote underneath: Conan, car thief.

It was seven o'clock. They would be waiting for me.

17

The album went from Dr Carvalho's hands to a foam manufacturer, look at the son of a bitch, it was him all right, the thieving son of a bitch, too bad they didn't put the son of a bitch's picture in the paper so I could spit on it, said the foam manufacturer, I'd love to spit on the son of a bitch. I popped a fistful of pistachio nuts into my mouth, took another shot of whiskey. I'd never had pistachio nuts before, I liked them. Six sons of bitches less, said the foam manufacturer, counting the corpses in the album. Eight, I corrected, two of them aren't there, Suel and Ezequiel. We laughed. Pistachio nuts. I liked Dr Carvalho's pleated pants. We're very pleased with you, Máiquel, that kid, that Conan, that little thief stole cars from a lot of people here in the neighborhood. A mahogany bar, mahogany dining table, mahogany bookcase, I liked it. He stole Dr Ricardo's car, Dr Marcelo's too. Pictures of flowers, I loved it. Dr Pedro's, Dr José Carlos's. Pictures of horses, loved it. The owner of the pharmacy there on the corner, what's the guy's name? Dried flowers, loved it. Pistachio. He stole his car too. A wooden duck, Dr Carvalho wanted to talk to me, but all I could hear was parts of sentences. A collection of crystal animals, loved it. Pictures from magazines, loved it. I looked at their faces, pretending I was listening, but what actually interested me most was looking at Dr Carvalho's house. I liked to cross my legs and think it was mine, that I lived there with Érica, that I was a dentist, hi, love, how was your day? Tiring, people have rotten teeth, just drink your whiskey, forget about everything, eat some pistachio nuts, the cook's making turkey à la California, I loved turkey à la California, and now they've come up with pizza à la California too, which is great, the other day I went to buy a lock, the foam manufacturer said, and the locksmith told me: you can install locks wherever you want, but it won't do any good, think about it, he makes his living selling locks.

I excused myself and left the living room, they thought I was going to the bathroom but I went into the hall leading to the bedrooms. The TV room. Office. I couldn't resist and took a peek at Dr Carvalho's bedroom. Everything in mahogany, they love mahogany. And cherry too. And Riga pine, they love it. A lot of gilded things. I got curious about the nightstand drawers. Check-books, credit cards, I'd never held a credit card in my hands.

I heard noises, tried to hide, before I could do anything, Gabriela came in, wrapped in a towel. I jumped onto her, afraid she'd scream. We fell, bang, the towel came off, I put my hand over her mouth, bang, the tramp didn't move, she didn't hide her breasts, didn't clench her legs, she didn't do anything. I thought, bang, sink my teeth, bang, tear off pieces, I took my hand from her mouth and she continued looking at me with those crazy eyes that certain actresses have, actresses who end up killing themselves. What do you want with me?

she asked. I got up, my hands were stuck in my pockets, one of them fingering the packet of cocaine I'd just bought. I took it from my pocket. I came here to give you this, wolf lady, and I left. She came after me, hey, what's this wolf lady story? Listen, man, I'm not going to listen to anything, goodbye, wolf lady. Bang.

Sit here, I'm going to tell you a story, Dr Carvalho said. I was afraid they'd seen my hard-on, Dr Carvalho's credit card and check-book were still in my pocket, how was I supposed to get them back to the bedroom?

They talked about a guy who stole television sets. I was worried about Gabriela, nonsense, the wolf lady liked to snort, she wasn't about to tell her father anything, my cock, now that was a problem, the credit card, I decided I'd stick it beside the sofa cushion as soon as I got a chance. That's what I'd do. But then the foam manufacturer's cellular rang and I got detoured, telephone, blender, beep, mixer, whatever, it astonishes me to think that somebody invented that, a plane flying through the air, a fridge, a phone without a cord, without anything, try it, he said, call someone. I didn't have anyone to call, I dialled Mr Humberto's shop, I was sure he wasn't there. Hello, he answered, it's me, Máiquel, Máiquel, you piece of shit, you son of a bitch, you think you own this place? I'm warning you, I'm taking these absences out of your pay, you filthy son of a bitch, I'm going to fire you. He was drunk. You look like a horse, he said that once to a woman who came to buy food for her dog, he let the animals out of their cages, he went out into the street to give anyone passing a hard time, gin, an entire bottle of gin, you stinking faggot, he told the pizza delivery boy, and the only reason the guy didn't beat the hell out of him was that I stepped between them and caught the blows in his place. Dr Carvalho and the foam manufacturer looking at me, at the cellular, at the clock, you're fired, he said, and slammed down the phone in my ear. I turned off the machine, worried, quickly got the basic information about my next assignment, said I'd take care of it right away, and left.

When I got to the shop, Mr Humberto was slumped over the counter, his head bleeding, a large cut, near the eyebrow. That cow, he said, that cow killed me. I went to the bathroom, wetted the end of a towel, cleaned the wound, he was calm, he was always calm after taking a beating. I straightened things, picked up the broken glass, and took Mr Humberto home. He wanted me to put him to bed, tell the cow not to hit me, he said as I covered him. She was in the doorway, waiting for me to beat it, Dona Maria, I said, I don't want you hitting your husband anymore. Oh, you don't, do you? No, I said. And what are you going to do if I crack the skull of that piece of crap who's not even worth throwing in the river? I'll kill you, I said. She wasn't expecting that, she showed no reaction. He pulled me down and kissed me on the forehead, my son, he said. I thought I hadn't heard right, what did you say? I said you're a filthy son of a bitch, he answered.

I left with my heart heavy, my eyes watering. My son. It wasn't till I was halfway home that I remembered Dr Carvalho's credit card and check-book were still in my pocket. My son. An unused check-book, twenty checks. A gold card. My son. Mr Humberto called me his son.

18

É rica wasn't home, it was always like that, after a quarrel she'd disappear. I turned on the TV and waited, ten glasses in the sink, cigarette ash on the floor, I got the broom and started sweeping. Érica had nothing to do with Cledir. Sandals on the stove, I put them away. Cledir was calm. Frying pan with egg stains, I washed it. Nothing but water and onions in the fridge. Cledir was very clean, liked white things, white Formica, she was peace, a peace outside myself, on the sidewalk, me sweeping, peace on the sidewalk and me, dirty, inside the home.

I heard Érica's laughter, I went outside. The sound was coming from the neighbor's house. I put my face against the window, she was talking with Marlênio.

Marlênio was an invisible pastor, I always had to make a tremendous effort to see him on the street and say hello. He lived with his mother and was always chasing God in his greasy suit. He invited me in, his mother offered coffee, I said no thanks, let's go, Érica. I'm talking to Marlênio, she said, I'm going to see the Powerful Heart of Jesus church. I have to talk to you, Érica. Some other time, today I'm going to church. We can go to the church tomorrow, the pastor said. Not tomorrow, Érica grabbed my arm and pulled me toward the door, I'll be back, Marlênio, I'm going to the church today. Wait for me.

We went into the house and she started in on how it wouldn't do any good for me to ask, to beg, it wouldn't do the least bit of good, she didn't want to have anything to do with me. I cleaned the house, see? Marlênio is a very good man, she said. I laughed, Marlênio is a pissant. He was talking about God, you idiot, you don't know the first thing about God. Marlênio is a philosopher, he lectured me about the seven deadly sins, do you by any chance even know the names of the seven deadly sins?

I started singing: Onward Christian soldiers, marching as to war, Érica hit me in the chest, you can laugh, she said, I'm a different woman, I don't pay any attention to those stupid prejudices. I'm going to tell you something, I was twelve years old, I woke up in the cab of my father's truck, that truck called ugly-and-from-far-away, remember? I woke up in the truck and I was alone in the cab, I got out, calling for my father. Know where my father was? At the side of the road, on the ground. I saw blood, lots of blood, I saw he wasn't breathing. Know what I did? I remembered a film I saw on TV, the woman was always getting fucked, and she'd had enough, she raised the sword, she didn't have a sword, I don't know why I said sword, she'd had enough and said to the sky: I'm never going to be hungry again. I did the same thing, nothing in this world will have the power to make me suffer, I said, never again, nobody, never, I promised, and that's what happened. You killed Suel, I didn't tear out my hair, I didn't turn you in to the police, I didn't weep in the gutter, I went after you and said: Take care of me. And you did. And you got married, I didn't throw myself off a cliff. I went on being your girl, I taught you a bunch of stuff, we had a lot of fun. But that day you left me on the street corner, when I was dying to see the Karate Kid, was too much, just too much. I said to myself: I may go hungry, but I won't put up with this, enough, go away. I'd rather be by myself. I'd rather hear Marlênio talk about God, I'm in real need of God.

Érica put on dark glasses, she was crying and didn't want me to see. I felt a great love for her, I love you, I said, no, you don't, I do, I love you a great deal. What do you want? You want me to cut off my arm? I'll cut it off. Want me to cut off my left leg? I'll cut it off. I'll cut off my dick if that's what you want. You won't cut off anything, you don't do anything for me. I moved toward her, I'll do whatever you want, she moved away, but I pressed her against the wall and could feel her heart beating, I'll slash my wrists, my feet, she bit me, kicked me, we fell down, I'll cut out my tongue, my fingers, I raised her skirt and entered her, I'll cut out my heart, she received me full of longing, whatever you want, I'll do it, I'll do anything, I want you to kill Cledir, she said. That's just what she said: I want you to kill Cledir.

We took a shower. Érica had an incredible ability to go from one extreme to the other, now she was happy, she laughed, I'm hungry, she said. We went to a restaurant, she ate, drank, and laughed a lot, I love laughing with you, she said, but I didn't laugh much that night. When I went to pay, I saw I didn't have enough money. I decided to use one of Dr Carvalho's checks. He wouldn't mind, and anyway I'd let him know.

19

On the 18th of January my daughter Samantha was born.

Eight pounds, one ounce of sugar, twenty-one inches long.

I held her in my lap, I'll take care of you, Samantha, a daughter needs her father.

I used another of Dr Carvalho's checks to pay for the toys, the blankets, the cradle, the baby clothes, the bottles, fifteen boxes of disposable diapers, and wrote on the stub: Don't forget to tell Dr Carvalho.

I wouldn't forget.

20

I hate you, you know.
I'm going to spend a few days at my cousin's, in Paraná.
I spit in your face.
Érica

The note was under the door. Lucky for me, Cledir was getting out of the taxi with Samantha and didn't see anything. We were returning from the maternity hospital, those four lines left me completely disoriented. Érica didn't have any relatives anywhere, I knew, she was furious with me because my daughter had been born, that's what it was.

I dropped everything and ran, ran and fell, fell and got up, got up and hoped and thought that the note was only a trick, but it wasn't a trick, Érica really had split and hadn't left a trail, not a piece of clothing in the closet. I also knocked at Marlênio's door, nobody answered. I went back there that night, the next day, Monday, Tuesday, Wednesday, nothing. Awful days. I wasn't inside myself, a horrible feeling, outside,

Érica in my every thought, the two of us fucking, in, pores, her asking me to kill Cledir, out, stories of husbands who kill their wives, in, wives who kill their husbands, out, I spent an entire night with the revolver in my hand, in, Cledir was asleep, out, with Érica I had no peace, out, I did everything on the run to be able to spend time with her and even if we stuck together like glue the whole time, in, it was too little, out, I wanted more, and even inside her, out, I wanted more, I wanted to enter, to unite, in, cross, out, I'll call you, she said, and I sat by the telephone all day long, out, and when we were going to meet, in, I would go through the entire day with a bomb inside me, out, it didn't explode, it protruded, in, and after every meeting I would wander around with my cock all raw, out, people spend their whole lives looking for love, and love is horrible, out, you know, I hate you, out, love is a detonator, spitting in the face, out, explosive charges, signed Érica, pain, I was exhausted, my liver was gone, out, I tore up the note and gave Érica up, truly gave her up, gave her up once and for all, Érica out.

I decided to concentrate all my efforts on work.

Name: Pedro Television. Twenty years old, mulatto. Pedro is a cruel man, Dr Carvalho said. Be cruel with him. I will.

Júlio, a gynecologist, was the first to speak: It was ten at night, my wife was away, I was watching television, heard a noise on the ground floor and went downstairs. I found this young guy in the middle of the living room with a gun in his hand. He was very nervous and I told him to take whatever he wanted, I'm alone in the house, I'm not going to make any problems for you. He told me to sit on the sofa and, with the gun constantly pointed at my head, began setting aside the things he was going to steal. I'm being robbed, I said, the first time it's ever happened to me, you have to understand my nervousness, please, let me have a glass of whiskey. He said no, but then he changed his mind and poured a whiskey for me and one for himself. I was sitting there quietly, drinking the whiskey, when I saw he was going to take a painting that my grandmother gave me, a landscape of Buriti Alegre, the city where she was born. I said: That painting isn't worth anything, you won't be able to sell it, take that other one, it's by Alexandre Costa, it's worth about four hundred dollars, it was of some wonderful parrots, those you see on the wall over there. He took my advice, and from then on that's how things went, me advising him on what to steal, the most valuable engravings, the crystal, the silver, everything. Suddenly, he sat down beside me and we started talking. He said he was really fucked, that his wife was pregnant, that he hated robbing, that he came from Bahia, and so on and so on, that old tale of woe that we're all familiar with. He was working as a stonecutter's helper, and he got fired for showing up ten minutes late. Érica, I love you. He seemed to be suffering, said the gynecologist. I felt I could control the situation, and I started talking about what a dirty deal social injustice was, those crooked politicians, all that stuff, in the days when I believed such nonsense, today I say fuck them, for my part, the government ought to build a wall at the Minas Gerais border and the northern part of the country can just fuck itself. Leave the poor there, let them roast to death in the north-east. I hate Ceará. I hate folklore. I hate blacks. But that's beside the point, the point is that he was calming down, the robber was calming down, telling stories, jokes, we laughed, soccer, and the night went by like that. We emptied an entire bottle. Around five in the morning, he said to me: I'm leaving, I'm not taking anything, you're a cool guy, I'm leaving. At least take the lighter things, I said;

he didn't want to, but I insisted. Take this portable TV, take this cash, I can hardly believe what I'm telling you, but it's the gospel truth. He said he was going away empty-handed, told me goodbye, hugged me, all right!, he said. When he got to the door, he stopped, looked me in the eye, took out the gun and said: This is so you won't think I'm one of the good guys, and bang, bang. He hit me with two shots. I lay there bleeding, and the only reason I didn't die was because I was able to drag myself to the gate and a neighbor found me bleeding on the sidewalk.

Maybe because of Érica's absence, I began to dedicate myself more to all that filth, began to enjoy hearing those putrid stories. I would hear them and it was like giving a chunk of meat to my hatred, then another chunk, I was becoming addicted to it. The exercise really works, I hate, he hates, we hate. On Monday, Érica still hadn't returned, nor Marlênio, the two of them together. Terrible days. I would wake up and go to a field to practice. I practiced and bought weapons, my arsenal, my collection, Tuesday, Érica away, rifles, bullets, Wednesday, I dreamed about Érica, her and Marlênio fucking in heaven, 9mm automatics, thirty-two rounds, shotguns. Thursday, loneliness, Friday I decided to change my strategy and not kill anybody without warning anymore. I had Gonzaga draw a skull and crossbones on cardboard and write above it: Santa Claus says Pedro Television will be the next to be sent to hell. Be warned: the angel is flying low. That didn't mean anything, it was just to create a mood. Sunday, always the saddest day, Gonzaga put the poster on the counter of the bar. People liked it.

Pedro Television heard about it, people told me. Somebody told me he was getting up money to split, to head north. I moved my plans forward, got everything ready for Saturday.

On Friday, I was working at the shop when I received an anonymous phone call, a woman saying that if I wanted to catch Pedro Television, he was holding up a house on Good Shepherd Street, number 45. Érica and the pastor.

Marcão, Enoque and I arrived there in two cars and stationed ourselves around the house, waiting for the thieves to come out. I placed the personnel at strategic points and then, together with Marcão, rang the neighbor's bell. A startled Italian guy opened the door, do you have your neighbor's phone number? He did. I dialed, someone answered. Put Pedro Television on, I said. Silence. It was Pedro Television himself who'd answered. OK, you son of a bitch. This is Máiquel speaking. I'm going to kill you today. All I'm waiting for is for you to come out of there.

I hung up the phone, went to the front of the house, and waited. A few minutes later, the light in the living room went out. Someone peeked out through the curtains. I raised my fist and showed the weapon. Marcão did the same. We waited a long time, nothing happened. Suddenly, three police vehicles arrived, twelve men got out and surrounded the house. Pedro Television came out, his hands in the air, followed by his two companions. The old couple came next, and the woman fainted as soon as she saw the police.

Pedro Television, as he was being searched, said there was a group of killers trying to get him. They're out there, they want to kill me. The detective ignored him, shoved the guys into the car, and drove away.

At Gonzaga's bar, my men told the story and laughed. I didn't want to drink. I went home with it stuck in my throat, stretched out on the sofa, tortured by rage.

The next day, I got the group together and went to the precinct, paid Pedro Television's bail. The jailer told me later that Pedro, when he found out it was me who'd put up the bail money, kneeled on the floor, begging in the name of God to let him stay in the cell. The animal walked out terrified, looking right and left, I let him go three blocks and then we threw the son of a bitch in the car.

We took him to a deserted street in the Capão Redondo district.

He asked me if he could pray. Pray, I said, but it won't do any good. He turned his back, looking at the sky. It was the last time he saw the sun.

21

Dr Carvalho, I used five checks from your check-book, here's the total, you can deduct it from my payment. I think your house is pretty, I wanted to see the bedroom, I opened the night-table drawer, the credit card was there, Gabriela came in, I thought she would think I was robbing you, I stuck the credit card in my pocket, and the check-book, I was going to return them but I left without doing it. The speech was on the tip of my tongue, I was about to speak, but then the maid came in with a tray of coffee, it was a different maid, what happened to the woman who used to work here? I asked. I sent her away, Dr Carvalho said, she stole my check-book. And a credit card also.

That was wrong. I ought to have felt sorry for the woman, ought to have said it was my fault, ought to return the check-book, but in those days that sort of thing happened a lot: something inside me screaming and something else, larger, ignoring. A wave coming from my stomach, weakly, and dying in my mouth, with no foam. Hatred, somebody once said, starts in the mouth. And that thing that I didn't know what it was and was already my own death, the beginning of my death, ended in my mouth, with no foam.

Now the bank calls me all the time, Dr Carvalho said, I stopped payment on the checks, they call from restaurants, from baby shops, she just had a baby, the ignorant thing, I wanted to give her a scare, you could do that for me, but my wife doesn't want to, she says it wasn't her, who was it then? It was her, I said, of course it was her, Dr Carvalho said, and for a moment we had nothing more to say, which made both of us uneasy. He looked at me in a strange way, I don't know how to explain it, only guys like him know how to look that way, rich people look that way, the poor look in a different way altogether. I lowered my head: I killed Pedro Television, I said, shhhh, keep your voice down, Máiquel, are you crazy? This is for you: Dr Carvalho handed me a box that the foam manufacturer had sent me, I opened it, a cellular telephone, for your work, he said. The foam manufacturer would pay the charges. But don't overdo it, Dr Carvalho said. The phone is for messages, use it for work.

I wasn't well, I didn't feel good, I was snorting a lot of coke, I wasn't sleeping and when I did sleep I felt like I was awake, I snorted, I didn't pay the slightest attention to my daughter, I would go to the shop every day, spend my time in the bathroom, snorting, I'd yell at Mr Humberto, I'd cry, listen to the radio, argue with Cledir, I phoned the girls on the XXX Hot Line, snorted, Máiquel loves Érica, Érica loves Máiquel, I'd write our names together inside hearts on tables at bars, arrows on trees and in the palm of my hand too. I snorted, went out with a few women, but women are all alike, they scream in bed, and I don't like women who scream in bed, I don't like women who give their opinion after fucking, I don't like women who call me my love, to hell with my love, I'm the killer.

One day I was at the shop, Érica comes in, white pants, white T-shirt, her hair wet, hi, I'm back. I could hardly speak. Cat got your tongue? She was so pretty and I was so wiped out, all in white and me in such pain, I'm out, I said, it's over, I said, she put the key to the house on the counter and said she didn't need it anymore, I'm going to live at the church, I'm going to work for the church. It was like a smack on the head, I felt dizzy. I was traveling with Marlênio, a gathering of the faithful in Paraná. A punch on the chin. You can't imagine how good it is to find God. A kick in the stomach. I began to laugh, shove God up your ass. Marlênio is good for me, I didn't want you to be annoyed, you know, I want a bit of peace. I turned my back and started arranging the pet food, dog food, I need a religion, she said, feed for horses, you told me that when you think you're going to die, that your daughter is going to die, that the trees are going to die, you can't even get out of bed, you cry, fish food, you cry at night, when you lay on the ground, in the woods, and see the stars, and see you're going to die, the infinite, you cry, Máiquel, and you cry when you wake up in the middle of the night and think you're going to die, that one day everything will end, you cry about it, you cry because you don't know, Máiquel, that God is the one true path for leaving here, God is the path to Heaven. Go fuck yourself, Érica. I've learned that people can die with a song on their lips, she said, mule feed, for stupid people, you can soften your heart, Máiquel. Feed, feed, feed. Are you going to stay a fool for the rest of your life? Yes, but not the kind of fool who spends his life in church, I answered. Rabbit food. She turned and left, I went on arranging the food and crying, all day.

That week Dr Carvalho called five times on the cellular and Gonzaga gave me another pile of messages, people who wanted my services, but I couldn't do anything except suffer. Érica and her new boyfriend Jesus, the asshole, I wonder if they do much fucking.

One day I couldn't take it anymore, I followed Marlênio to the church, discovered where she lived. A hall with a corrugated roof, blue and white stripes, it looked like a dance hall. God Is Light was written in red, daily worship services: seven am and seven pm. The faithful had to show a card to get in, and Érica stamped the card. I went there every day to watch her. She cleaned the church, collected money from the faithful and stamped their cards, while I snorted and suffered. Marlênio was leaving, they hadn't fucked that night. Nor the next night, or the next, they never fucked, they talked a lot, but she always went to bed by herself and the greaseball went home to sleep with his mother. Shit, how that made me happy.

I want to talk to you, Érica. I asked her to come back.

She said no. She wanted to stay with God. Máiquel, I need something, I can't say what it is, it must be God, I'm trying, there must be something, I kneeled at her feet, begging, crying, don't get on your knees, she said, I don't deserve it, she said she didn't deserve for me to kneel, you deserve everything, I'm going to do whatever you want, but she said she didn't want anything, she just wanted to get that pain out of her heart. What pain, Érica, what pain do you have in your heart? She went into the church without explaining what the pain was.

I was so desperate that I started running, running, I'm going to run till I die, I thought, till I explode, till I fly, and I ran, and I arrived home and locked myself in the bedroom and snorted. Cledir began to bang on the door, open up. I pushed the dresser to block the entrance, open up, open the door, open this door, open this door, open this door, open this door, I opened it. She began to scream at me, I listened to it all, understood it all, she was frightened, the hatred began right in my mouth and exploded in my brain and exploded into my hands and I gripped Cledir's throat, squeezed, squeezed, squeezed and only stopped when I heard the bones in her neck snap.

22

My father once told me a story he read in a detective novel by a very famous writer. I never forgot that story, pay attention, this is important. A woman goes to a private detective, her husband had left work to get something to eat and never returned. He was a good man, honest, had never cheated anyone, not even in his own family, which incidentally wasn't very well off; in other words, the idea that he ran off with a case full of money was out. There was another possibility, desertion, but everything indicated that the couple was happy, no fights, the guy was a good husband and a good father, there was no reason for him to leave the family. They looked for the man everywhere, hospitals, police stations, everywhere you can imagine, all the cities, everything, a really absurd story, the guy had evaporated, with no motive, with no explanation.

Some years later, the detective in the story, this happens in the United States, the detective finds the man in a small town, I don't know how he finds the guy, I just know he found him. Hey, man, you've been gone for years, your wife's suffered like crazy, what the devil happened? By then the guy had another life, another family, another job. Here's what he said: I was going to get something to eat, I was walking along, and as I was passing by a construction site a block of cement, or something, but I think it was cement, fell right beside me, it could have fallen on my head, but it fell right beside me. It was as if someone had opened the cauldron of life and stuck my head in it, as if someone was telling me, look how this crap works.

That was how it was, the man stuck his face in the cauldron of life and everything lost its meaning. His wife, the children, work, because those things don't have any meaning, they only have meaning when we stick our head in the cauldron and see that life is like that, living and dying. He walked away and never came back.

I'm telling you this story to show you that people really do vanish. For some good reason, for no reason at all, they leave children, money, they leave anything. Lots of people disappear, just read the papers. People go to the corner to buy bread and evaporate. He was playing in front of the house and disappeared. She went to school and never returned. And that doesn't mean they were murdered by their husbands. That's what I'm trying to tell you: people disappear.

Érica was exactly like that. You you you are a locust, a cloud of locusts, you screw up my life, you couldn't do this to me, you're a fool, I thought she was going to say all that when I knocked at the church door, in the early morning, desperate, saying that I had killed Cledir. I thought she was going to become desperate, start talking about Jesus, about Marlênio. She did all that, just like I'd imagined, but then she sat on the bed and stopped crying and made a plan to save me. We were in the room where she lived, a cubicle with a bed, a work table, a water glass. Samantha was asleep on my lap.

This is what's going to happen, people will go there looking for her, the family, girlfriends, neighbors, the police, and you're going to tell them: She left me. She disappeared, didn't leave a note. They're used to such things. The police will suspect you, everybody will, but so what? Suspicion is just suspicion. They'll have to find the corpse. They'll have to get witnesses. You said no one saw it. Or did someone? No, I answered.

I did everything she ordered. I borrowed Marcão's car and we went to the house. Samantha cried the whole time, and that made me nervous. We left everything in order, then put Cledir's body in the trunk of the car.

Samantha was asleep in the back seat, we drove for a long time, went into the Cantareira hills, I wanted to bury Cledir in the forest, deep in the forest. We stopped along the highway, and when I was taking Cledir's body out, a truck passed. The man stopped, Érica leaped out of the car. Any problem? he asked. A flat tire, I said. Need any help? No, we just changed it, Érica said. The man left and I thought my heart would explode. I went into the forest carrying Cledir, dug a deep hole, six feet, threw Cledir's body in it, replaced the dirt.

We returned home without a word. Midway, I remembered the locust, why did you say I'm a locust? I asked. Because of your antennas, she said. What do you mean? Samantha was showing signs of waking up, she motioned for me to be quiet.

When we got home, Érica put Samantha in her cradle. We went to bed. Érica said she smelled a good scent on the pillow, was it her smell? I said it was, and Érica tossed and turned, unable to get to sleep. I couldn't sleep either, I was thinking about Cledir's body, the dirt covering her face, that was what left the biggest impression on me, the dirt falling on her face. The truck driver. Érica said it was strange to sleep in that bed. I asked if she wanted to live with me. She said yes, she'd go and fetch her clothes the next day. You're very good for me, I said. We started kissing, the image of the truck driver wouldn't leave my head. He might have written down the plates of my car. Someone would discover the body. Newspapers. The truck driver would tell of the couple in a metallic-brown Dodge Dart. I got up. I'm going back, I said.

I went. I dug up the corpse, put it in the trunk, and brought it home. I didn't think it was safe to leave Cledir in the car, I had a cold, so I couldn't smell anything, but she might already have begun to smell. When Érica saw me come in carrying Cledir, she began to cry. She's so dirty, poor thing. I'm going to wrap her up, I said, bring some bags from the kitchen. What bags? Érica asked. Érica screamed at me, garbage bags, is that what you mean? You're going to put the woman in a garbage bag? Look at her face, look at how unhappy she is, look at the two of us here, fucked. Stop it, Érica. I won't stop. Érica wanted to bathe Cledir, I thought it was absurd, but Érica was hysterical, screaming, I was afraid the neighbors would hear, so I agreed. We went to the bathroom, removed Cledir's clothes, Érica soaped her while I held her beneath the shower. Even dead she's pretty, Érica said, she has a pretty body, don't you think? Let's get this over with, I said. Did you fuck her, Máiquel? Stop it. Did you fuck or not? I didn't reply. Érica threw water at me. Answer, you fool. Sometimes, I said. What does sometimes mean? It means exactly that: sometimes. You bastard, you fucked her every day, as soon as I left you you started fucking her.

Érica hit me in the chest and left the bathroom, slamming the door. I stayed there, alone with the soapy Cledir, I got a towel, dried Cledir, took the corpse to the living room, Érica was there, pouting on the sofa. Where are we going to put Cledir? Throw her in the street, she said. Érica, you're jealous of a person who's dead, I'm not jealous, yes, you are. I'm going to leave her in the kitchen, I said. No, Érica said, it's better to put her under the bed.

I didn't think that was right, but we put Cledir under the bed.

I collapsed on the bed, exhausted. I was feeling very bad. It was strange. Érica climbed on top of me, I didn't want to, we fucked. Afterwards, Érica slept and I spent the rest of the night looking at her face.

Érica never did explain to me why she'd called me a locust. I wasn't a locust.

23

W e're worse than Baltimore and Houston, we're worse than New York and Los Angeles, we're second only to Rio de Janeiro and Johannesburg, but Johannesburg has a hundred homicides per 100,000 inhabitants, that's right, one hundred, and we're almost halfway there, we'll get there soon if things continue as they are.

It was the big guy speaking, his quivering gut hanging over his pants, we were drinking whiskey. They caught me at the gate, I was leaving to bury Cledir, they caught me by surprise, it was horrible. I just stopped by to introduce you, said Dr Carvalho, and he added that the big guy had wanted to meet me for some time, you two need to have a talk. Dr Carvalho didn't even let me say anything, Dr Carvalho is that me-me-me type, he never listens to anything, he drove away and left me at the door of my house with the big guy, who was a police detective. I suggested we talk at Gonzaga's bar, I didn't want him going in the house, Érica would be startled. I'll follow you, I said, the big guy said it'd be better if we went in my car. I'm out of gas, he said. He didn't even give me time to think, he got into my car, into Marcão's car, I mean, got in and sat down and Cledir in the trunk and me with a cold and not knowing whether or not she was smelling.

Want another whiskey? he asked and I said OK, we drank another whiskey. Look at this, he said, it was a newspaper, this is the cultural supplement, the most important cultural supplement in the country, and look here, know what that is? It was an ad for a pistol. That's an ad for a revolver, he said, indignantly, .38 caliber, this shows that people want to go around armed, everybody wants to have his own weapon, his club, every last one of them, people want to defend themselves, and then they add, important: use requires training and emotional stability, ha, emotional stability, that's a good one, people are terrified, people are buying guns even over the phone, and it's all going to get worse. I told you, we've overtaken New York, we've overtaken Baltimore, like I said, and now there are billboards saying don't use firearms. Yeah, don't use firearms. Anyone who watches the news on TV runs out to buy a machine gun. It's in writing right here: we sell guns. Buy guns, don't use guns, what do they want from us? Tell me, what do they want? I don't know, I said, I know, he said, they want men like you. I've been following your work, my men talk about you a lot, I was the one who asked Carvalho to introduce us. People here in the neighborhood love you, and you know it. The businessmen respect you. The police respect you. The housewives respect you. And what is it you do, Máiquel? I killed people, but I didn't say that, I waited for him to answer. Philanthropy for the police, that's what you do. Philanthropy, I repeated, it's philanthropy, he said, except that in this country no one should be a philanthropist, always charge, charge a lot. I charge, I said, you charge too little, he said, you charge far too little, nobody wants to get their hands dirty, he said, there's a good market, he said, a really good market, a guy can make a lot of money from it.

We had another whiskey. Have you got a nice piece of meat there? he asked Gonzaga. Nice piece of meat, Dr Carvalho was like that too, meat every day, for me, Dr Carvalho said, for me meat has to be dripping blood, he always said that, the detective's beef was also dripping blood, making a pool of blood on the plate, a whole lot of blood. I want to propose a partnership, Máiquel, in a firm offering protection of property.

I felt something warm in my chest, a warm kind of peace, I don't know what came over me, it wasn't the whiskey, it was the detective's words which brought me that peace, that pride, a police detective offering to go into business with me; I really was a beloved person in the neighborhood, people would pass by and blow their horns, wave, I felt such peace, I felt like showing the detective Cledir's corpse, but I didn't, I thought it best not to.

We would provide security for the neighborhood: from the shantytown residents, do the arithmetic, if each shack pays five dollars, he said, the price has to be in dollars, the dollar, let's face it, is our true currency, five hundred shacks, two thousand five hundred dollars, that's nothing, it's peanuts, because there's also small businessmen, large businessmen, industrialists, multinationals, millionaires, multimillionaires, congressmen, the enemies of congressmen, arguments, the lovers of congressmen, lovers in general, husbands who get in the way of everything, wives who get in the way, business partners who get in the way, environmentalists, defenders of human rights, there's all that, everybody's going to want our services, he said.

Santana, that was the detective's name, Santana would come in with the office, the secretaries, the telephone, a plaque for the firm, the lawyer and, of course, he said, the power, the influence, the coverage. I would come in with myself, my team, with my know-how, he said. My name won't appear on the papers, he said, you know I'm a detective, and there's always some civilian, some congressman, lawyer, human-rights activist, there's always one of those types wanting to make trouble for a guy like me, like us. We'll put down the name of an acquaintance of mine. Don't worry, he won't be calling the shots, we'll be the ones calling the shots.

We shook hands, mine was already a bit numb from the alcohol.

I ran home, I wanted to tell Érica the news, let's celebrate, I said, and what does a property-protection firm do, she wanted to know, it does a lot of things, I said, basically a lot of things, where did you bury Cledir? Shit, I had forgotten to bury Cledir, she was still there, in the trunk.

I went to bury Cledir. I felt very good. I started digging the hole, I was fine, but I didn't have any strength, every time I stuck the shovel in the ground, my body lost its balance and I fell, I must have drunk a lot, it must have been late, past midnight, I lay down, closed my eyes, happy, what a pretty night, a property-protection firm, all those stars in the sky, security and belongings and a future and a business and money and security and belongings and all those stars in the sky, I fell asleep.

I woke the next day with the sun in my eyes, Cledir beside me and stiff as a board, a horrible thing. I was in Marcão's backyard, I don't know how that stupid idea had gotten into my head, but I remembered perfectly that I'd thought it was a good idea to bury Cledir in Marcão's yard, he'd gone to Santos and wouldn't be back till the next day. It was obvious that I ought to bury Cledir somewhere else, but that would mean keeping her in the trunk for who knows how much longer, all that tension, I couldn't take it.

They were giving me an opportunity, I couldn't do that sort of thing anymore. I ought to stop snorting, stop drinking, stop acting foolishly. They were giving me an opportunity, I had to take advantage of it. I was a lucky guy. Not everybody got an opportunity like this. That's what I thought as I was burying Cledir.

I also thought that I mustn't forget to let Mr Humberto know I wasn't going to be working there any longer. Mr Humberto was an all-right guy.

PART TWO

24

Arabesques and cashmeres from Russian folklore, huh, I like that, do you like it? I didn't even know what it was, I was shaving, Érica was sitting on the marble countertop in bra and panties, a decorating magazine in her hands, she was always looking at one of those magazines since we moved into the new apartment, three bedrooms, a master bedroom, double garage, swimming pool, party room, for just twenty-five percent you take on the mortgage and pay the balance in as many as a hundred and eighty months. Functional style, young style, Russian traditional, Érica was constantly saying such things, she liked to learn, she liked to make things up, to do, to buy, and my heart was filled to the top, overflowing, full of love, I was absolutely ready to give her everything she wanted, all right, Érica, do like they do in Russia, I went to the bedroom with her behind me, I also like Indian cane, you know that bamboo furniture? Bamboo is cool, I said, where's my navy-blue suit? Érica opened the wardrobe and took out the suit, suits go on this side, she said, I was going to have a full day, that piece of crap, a repulsive little guy, public transportation business, I was very polite, I went to the trouble of going there, the idiot left me cooling my heels, saw me very reluctantly, our firm provides protection for over thirty industries, I said, we have a specialized team, I did a lot of talking. We have our own system, he said, I don't need your services, he said, that gringo idiot was going to see a thing or two. Cledir's aunt called again, Érica said, she screamed at me on the phone.

Érica had put the magazines aside, she was lying on the bed, her head resting in her hands, a sad expression, I wasn't paying much attention to Érica those days, I lay down beside her, Érica, forget Cledir, her aunt can yell, she can threaten, everything's under control, don't worry. I'm not worried, she said, I feel guilty. Guilty? I said, you're not guilty of anything. Yes I am, and when Samantha cries I feel more than guilt, it burns, it hurts, I feel a hole inside me when I see that trunk full of clothes she wore, shoes. You haven't thrown them out yet? I asked. I can't bring myself to do it, she said, I feel pity, one day I tried on a white T-shirt of hers. It had Be happy, Be happy on it. You don't even understand English to know how sad that is.

Everything was going fine, the office was going fine, I was making a potful of dough, the mortgaged apartment was in a great location, Samantha was getting used to Érica, I used all those arguments. That's what it is, she said, things were never so good, I feel that something is deceiving us, to have it so good like this is the proof that we're going to end up completely fucked.

Érica had a sadness inside her, a ready sadness waiting for a reason to explode, she would go back and forth, there were days when she'd wake up and dance around our bed, and suddenly, I have no idea why, she would lock herself in the bedroom and cry, she'd cry before going to sleep, cry in the shower, cry watching television, let's have some coffee together, I said, let's get away this weekend, let's go to that hotel you saw on television, Érica became excited, you swear? I swear, I swear, we went to have coffee in the dining room, the glass-top table just like Dr Carvalho's, I insisted on that, it let us see our feet, my shoes gleamed, Érica was wearing a pair of white slippers with a cluster of feathers, I sat there staring at that tuft of feathers and eating papaya. Ubatuba, she said, I hope it doesn't rain.

The doorbell rang, I opened the door, it was Marlênio, the same cheap suit, the same idiotic face, I was dying to knock Marlênio around a bit. Érica was happy to see him, come in, Marlênio, you're going to love my new apartment, look at the view, let's go downstairs, I want to show you the pool, did you bring your swimming trunks? I took Érica to the office, what kind of story is this? I asked. I invited Marlênio to swim in the pool, she said. I don't like the guy. Érica said she was going to give some money to his church. What? You're going to give money to that guy? To his church, she said. Érica, love, I said, or rather I wanted to say, but I was so mad the words wouldn't come out, I felt like shoving my fist in Érica's face, give my money to that exploiter of patsies, swimming in my pool. I turned my back and left, went through the living room without looking at Marlênio, go with God, the asshole said. I slammed the door as hard as I could. Sooner or later Marlênio would get what was coming to him.

Alpha – Security Services and Property Surveillance Ltd, I liked the name, I also liked the logo, a circle with a dot in the center, a target, Santana had thought that up. Alpha was twenty blocks from my apartment, on Ferreira Soares, a busy area in the Santo Amaro district, full of commercial offices and shops.

I got out of the car and looked at the street, two girls in shorts waiting for a bus, the taller one smiled at me, women like guys in suits, like guys who drive a black two-door Opala with mag wheels, I was noticing that, women looked at me.

I climbed the side stairs that led to the office. Fátima, my secretary, was there, yawning. Am I sleepy, she said, there's a young girl inside waiting to speak to you. A young girl, who is it?

It was Gabriela, she was sitting at my desk, drawing, you know this guy? I took the paper, it was me, my face she'd drawn, OK, Gabriela, what do you want? I want coke, she said. I've told you a thousand times, I don't deal coke, Gabriela. She closed her eyes, with a disheartened expression, rolled up her sleeves, showed her arms, they were covered with needle marks, look, Máiquel, I used to be super-insecure, I thought I was zero minus, and that day you stole my father's check-book, hold on, I said, I didn't steal a goddamn thing, it's true, she said, you didn't steal my father's check-book, I was wrong, I'm sorry, you're forgiven, anyway, she said, that day you didn't steal my father's check-book you gave me the magic dust, I tried it, I liked it, I liked it. Look here, girl, if you're trying to say again that I'm to blame for the terrible shape you're in, no, she said, no, no way, you're not to blame for anything, I'm grateful to you, you saved me, she said, you're a kind of of of godfather, don't give me that, Gabriela, all right, I won't give you that, but you know, she said, those things help a person, everything's lighter, without the magic dust I shake, my tongue gets balled up, I had to go to hospital, you know, those things are expensive, you know,

I flunked, it's the second time I've had to repeat the year, my father has turned off the spigot and I'm going to take care of everything, I can pay you. I'm very sorry, Gabriela, I'm not a supplier. You've got it, I know you've got it, she said. Look here, Gabriela, go to Cocaine Users Anonymous, Crack Smokers Anonymous before you die, ciao, I pushed her out and locked the door; she knocked on it for a few seconds, Máiquel, help me, I heard the sound of her stylish clogs, punishing the wooden floors of the hallway, then I heard the outer door close. She must be going after Marcão. Lately it was always like that.

I looked for the envelope that Santana had said he'd leave in my drawer; it was there. Sidenil, mulatto, seventeen, Jardim Campinas district. He stole cigarettes and liquor from Carlos's bakery. Carlos, Carlos, Carlos, I remembered, Carlos was one of our clients. Quinho, seventeen, black, belongs to a gang of drug runners. Evaristo, thirteen. Just think, thirteen years old, lemon vendor, glue sniffer. Tried to steal Tito's wife's watch; Tito is an investigator.

Those cards were the way we worked. When a delinquent came through the precinct to be sent to the juvenile shelter, the investigators took a photo and wrote a card, where they put name, age, area of activity, and sent it to Alpha.

I told Fátima to call Enoque, gave him the cards, I'll handle this today, he said. Enoque asked if he'd have a car, ask Santana to arrange for one from the precinct, I said.

I opened the closet, took out my .38, it had been a long time since I'd done any street service, I had a team of forty men working for me, but with some things there was no other way, I had to take care of it myself. I called three men to go with me.

★   ★   ★

Hands up, everybody on the floor.

The bar was on a dirt road near the Billings dam.

I walked among the people, all of them on the floor, only the women were making any noise, the cows, they can't control themselves. The one I was looking for was near the snooker table, you, I said, come with me. The young guy didn't get up, I kicked him in the stomach, and even then he didn't want to get up. My men put him in my car. I'm sticking to our deal, he said, I'm out of your area, I'm not in the game, he said, shut up, I said, and began looking for a place where I could stop the car, a small soccer field, no one around, I stopped. Listen, man, I said, here's what you're going to do, you're going to get that bunch of shitasses of yours together and you're going to hit that gringo's bus company, on Tobias Menezes, you're going to hit it tonight, and tomorrow night too, kill the watchman, half of what you find there is mine, I want that son of a bitch gringo, you read me? I got a job, I'm out, look at my work card. I looked. Office boy in a steel company. So what are you doing here? It's my lunch hour. All right, I said, you have a time to sleep, don't you? You'll do the job on your off-time. Or are you going to let me down?

Verli, he had that funny name, I don't know if it was his first name or his surname. Verli was fucked, a third-rate shit of a thief. One day, kneeling at my feet, with my revolver pointing at his head, he said: Dolores, save me. What did you say? I asked. Dolores, my mother's name, he said. Our mothers had the same name, Dolores, I thought that had some kind of significance, I told him to piss off, disappear from the neighborhood, I said, or I'll blow your brains out next time.

Verli agreed to do the job for me.

140

25

I passed a truck, the highway was free, the sky was blue, Érica put a tape in the player, we made our way calmly down a road full of curves.

A weekend in Ubatuba, the Hotel Miranda, double bed, flowered bedspread, hair dryer in the bathroom and all those little bottles of shampoo and foam and creme and ocean view, wonderful breakfast, a ten-foot table with all sorts of cold cuts, fruit, jellies, cheese, lots of varieties.

In the morning, the beach.

We had lunch at the Enseada Restaurant, I had crab. In the afternoon, we went to the shopping mall, Érica bought two hats, three dresses, and a crawling doll for Samantha. We had a double scoop of ice cream with hot fudge topping. And an ice-cream float too.

That night, Érica wanted to see the Tropical night club, stroboscopic lights, real coconut palms, the waiters, or rather, the waitresses dressed like Hawaiians, you buy a necklace when you go in and the necklace's beads are the same as money, you buy drinks with them, whatever you want,

Érica and I drank cuba libres, Érica was wearing her new red dress, clinging to her body, sleeveless, her hair combed back, you're beautiful, we kissed in the middle of the dance floor, those lights blinking, look, Érica said, let's knock off this kissing business, I want to dance, can't you see that? Two hours later we were back at the hotel, each inside the other, how lucky I am, she said, how lucky I am, I repeated. We fucked till dawn.

26

Sunday night, returning from Ubatuba.

I played back the answering machine, there were five messages.

Máiquel, this is Santana, call me, it's important. The other messages were from Santana too, all saying the same thing in a tone of voice that was more and more troubling. I called him, we set up a meeting for half an hour later.

I showered, shaved, left Érica in front of the television, bring back a pizza, she yelled as I was getting into the elevator, and some Coca-Cola too.

Santana was waiting for me on the sidewalk, as soon as I got out of the car he gave me the news: Marcão had been arrested with three kilos of cocaine. Fucking hell, I said.

Let's get him a lawyer, I said. I've done that, Santana said, but it's just going through the motions, because Marcão is fucked, a lawyer is just window dressing, he was caught red-handed, there's no way around it. What do you mean there's no way around it? I asked. Just what I said, the arrest warrant has already been issued. You're a police detective, I said. I'm a detective, but I don't know if you've ever heard of something called the law. Yeah, I've heard of it, I said. That's how it is, he said, Marcão was caught in another jurisdiction, I can't do a thing. What about the detective in that jurisdiction? I've made inquiries, Santana said, the guy's not on the take. Not on the take? There's no such thing, the guy has to be on the take. Those are the facts, Santana said, the guy's not on the take. It happens.

Me and Marcão, facing each other, during prison visiting hours.

It was real strange, I got in the car, turned the corner, and ran into a roadblock, I'm certain somebody fingered me, real strange that roadblock, Marcão said.

He was wearing a beaten-up pair of sandals; I felt sorry for him.

Absolutely certain, somebody fingered me, Marcão continued. Who'd put the finger on you? I asked. Beats me, somebody who wants to fuck me. Who wants to fuck you? Beats me, Marcão said, I'm king of the hill now and if there's one thing that nobody can stand, it's seeing a guy get ahead in the world. Beaten-up sandals, I took another look. I'm a winner, he said, I've got a cool car, I've got money, nobody can stand that, a black guy with money in a cool car, a black guy going into a restaurant, a black guy making it and laughing, they won't tolerate it, they go mad with hate, that's the reality, he said, we hope that people, including our friends, have a real dumb crappy life, or end up in the gutter for good, so we won't have to run into them making it, because all of us, every one of us human beings can't stand the success of another human being, we hate Pelé, he said. I don't hate Pelé, I said. Me neither, Marcão said, I don't personally hate Pelé, you don't

144

personally hate Pelé, but our soul hates Pelé, we hate Pelé because he didn't die drunk and poor, eating turf, and we think that's decent, eating turf. How are you going to get me out of here? he asked me. I don't know, I said. You don't know, and that lawyer Santana sent is an imbecile, all the time saying I was caught red-handed, I know I was caught red-handed, he doesn't have to keep repeating it every five minutes.

Take it easy, Marcão. Take it easy my ass, I was caught doing a job for us, I was working, don't forget that, so don't think I'm going to rot in this stinking cell, 'cause I'm not.

What about the jailers here, I asked, have they got anything against making some dough?

Don't think it's that easy, don't think that it's just a matter of offering money to the jailers, said Santana, and he also said he was against it. I'm against it, absolutely against it. An escape like that will attract a lot of media attention, and the authorities, they'll go after Marcão and wind up here, at our door.

We were in my office, Santana was smoking at the window, he inhaled and blew out the smoke. I smell shit, I said; if Marcão keeps his trap shut there's no problem, Santana replied. No, I said, you don't understand, you must have stepped in dog shit. I was right. Santana got a sheet of newspaper from the desk, tore it, and began cleaning the mess.

The phone rang, line three for you, said Fátima, it's a gringo. Santana carried an enormous wallet, so thick it wouldn't fit in his pocket, or in his glove compartment. He wrapped the strap around his wrist and left, I'll call you later, he said.

I picked up the phone.

This is Leonel Aischer, I own a transport company, you were in my office last week offering your services.

Out the window, I saw Santana, limping, wiping his heel

on the sidewalk, trying to clean the sole of his shoe. I laughed. Ah, yes, of course I remember you. How are things?

At four that afternoon, Aischer was in my office. He was a changed person, not a bit like the arrogant guy who'd seen me so unwillingly the week before. We talked about dogs, I don't remember which of us brought up the subject, Dobermans, German bulldogs, Brazilian mastiffs, and boxers. I like the Rottweiler's style, I said, first he attacks, then he barks. We laughed. He said he was thinking of buying a Scottish terrier, you know, those black dogs, they're fleshy and have a bite like the German shepherd's, they're very good. The German shepherd is really good, I said, he does a hundred yards in seven seconds. You need a good trainer, he said. Yes, I said, but it's no good to just teach it to understand refs and aus. What? Refs and aus, I said, attack and forward. Ah, yes, he said. A dog needs affection, I said. Some people beat them, I'm against it, the animal can lose its character. You understand dogs, he said. I like dogs.

Aischer told me of his problem, his firm had been robbed twice since I had visited him. The watchman had been killed. I'm worried, he said.

I promised to send, that very night, three men to keep an eye on it. We agreed on everything, he signed a check.

When he got to the door, I gave him our poster: We co-operate with Alpha – Security Services and Property Surveillance Ltd. Put it on the door of your establishment, I said.

At five, I was on my way to meet Érica at the shopping mall. When I got onto Matias Severo to take the bypass, I noticed a crowd around Marcão's house. Two police wagons. Neighbors. I got out, made my way through the onlookers. In the yard, I saw some policemen removing the mortal remains of Cledir. They were looking for drugs, said one ugly woman to another ugly woman, and they found a corpse.

27

I woke up at four in the morning, I had the impression I'd heard voices, I went to the living room, found Érica stretched out on the floor, her feet resting against the wall.

Were you on the phone? I asked.

No, she said, I was saying a prayer of repentance. Do you know how to say a prayer of repentance?

No.

Dear Lord, I have great sorrow at having sinned, for I deserve punishment, I have offended Thee, my father and savior, forgive me, O Lord, I desire to sin no more.

Amen, I said. That part I know.

I had a funny dream, I dreamed I was at a discothèque, dancing, Cledir and me.

Want me to warm up a little milk? I asked. Milk helps you sleep.

We were dancing, holding hands, then Cledir said: Érica, you look like Jesus Christ. Get that picture that hung on the wall at my house and look closely, you'll see, your mouth is just like Jesus Christ's. And the color of your eyes too.

Only Cledir talked, I wanted to talk too, but every time I opened my mouth something white came out, a mist, I was afraid to. Then she said: We have a friend in common, she said, Jesus Christ is our friend, and it was him, Jesus Christ, in person, who commanded me to ask a favor of you: turn yourself in to the police.

You don't look like Jesus Christ, I said.

Yes, I do. The picture she was talking about is there on the dresser, in Samantha's room. Want to see it?

We tiptoed into Samantha's room. Érica picked up the picture, Jesus Christ, greenish, with his hands folded over his chest and those eyes like a harmless dog's.

Look at the mouth. Doesn't it look like mine?

Not in the least, Érica.

I'll cover up the beard so you can see better.

She covered up Jesus's beard.

Look how striking it is, she said.

It's Jesus Christ without a beard, that's all I see. Want me to warm up some milk?

What if they find out it's Cledir's body?

They're not going to find out, I said. You want some milk?

Yes. Chocolate milk.

I went to the kitchen, made chocolate milk, and returned to the living room. Érica was still looking at the picture of Jesus.

Give that to me, I said.

I took the picture and put it in the trash can and then I called Érica. We went to bed, hugging.

I have to tell you something, Érica said. I told Marlênio that we killed Cledir.

★   ★   ★

I went into the church and sat in one of the rear pews. My watch said eight o'clock. No one was there. I tried to remember the prayer of repentance. I couldn't.

A guy came into the church carrying a broom. It was Marlênio, it took me a time to recognize him. We're closed, he said as soon as he saw me. I said Érica wasn't well, she asked me to come and get you.

We got into my car, he asked me if we'd spoken to the police. No, I said. When are you going to give yourselves up?

I took the bypass, this isn't the way to your house, he said. Érica's at my aunt's, I answered. A few minutes later, two drops of sweat appeared on his shirt. When I turned onto one of those muddy roads, the fog got thicker and I saw he was trembling.

We got out of the car and stood for a few minutes looking at a dense thicket in front of us. I could smell rain. I know that you priests can't go around telling what you've heard in confession. I'm not a priest, Marlênio said, I'm a pastor, a pastor, a pastor. Érica promised me you were going to turn yourselves in. I gave her two days.

I gave her two days, that was what disoriented me. Pastor. I hit him in the face, he fell, and when he got up, his lip cut, punch, he said we should confess to the police, punch, repent our faults, punch, and our sins, punch, we'd be saved and escape, punch, the fires of hell. I hit him in the face again, and even on the ground he went on vomiting Bible verses, that God did not mean us for wrath, I didn't let him complete the sentence. I jumped on top of Marlênio, God is slow to anger, he said, and a storm exploded inside me, and my lightning bolts smashed Marlênio's bones, and I flashed blood and thundered blood until every muscle in my body begged me to stop.

I've already got God's forgiveness, Marlênio. And if God still thinks I owe anything, I'll come back and kill you.

I got in the car and left.

When I got to the office, Santana was waiting for me. That fool black is going to be the end of us, he said, did you know they found a corpse in Marcão's backyard? I just found out, I said.

It might have been a good idea to tell Santana everything, but I was tired, my arms ached, my legs ached, and I'd seen Ezequiel's mother crossing the street opposite Alpha a few minutes earlier and that made me remember the vow I'd broken, I'd sworn I'd send her money every month, I never sent any money at all, never even remembered the promise made at Ezequiel's tomb. She crossed the street, calm, with the face of a good person, proper, she never saw me, doesn't know who I am, I felt like greeting her, how is your pain? You've got blood on your shirt, Santana told me. Where were you? I ran over a dog, I answered.

A corpse messes things up, Santana said, it's a woman, a friend at the coroner's office told me. The detective handling the case is a bear, he called in an expert who's a real fire-eater, they're going to identify the body, mark my words, do you know who the woman is? No, I said. Was it one of our jobs? Santana asked. How should I know? I answered. I'm going to visit Marcão today, I said. Like hell you are, leave that to me, I'll take care of it, Santana protested.

After Santana left, I got even more agitated. Fire-eater. I called Érica, everything's all right, I said. She promised me she wouldn't do anything foolish, I promised her I wouldn't do anything foolish, we promised to go to the movies that night, and then we'll go get plastered, I said.

I was very nervous, twice I had the impression of seeing Ezequiel's face in the crowd crossing my path, at first I thought it was because I hadn't slept, but then, immediately, I ran into Ezequiel's mother at the door to my office, I thought somebody, I don't know who, some invisible something was against me, I believed in that, in the invisible, in hell, I always knocked on wood three times, I didn't walk under ladders, I didn't laugh on Fridays, didn't use the number 13, didn't spill salt at the table, didn't do any of those things.

I got my car, went out for a drive, drove around at random saying aloud, my life is going fine, problems come and go because that's how life is, there's nothing mysterious about life and I can go on. I got out at Gonzaga's bar, I hadn't been there for some time. I ordered a vodka with ice and lime, sat there looking at passers-by, paying attention to their faces, I didn't see Ezequiel a single time and I took that as a good sign. A man sat down at my table, I'm a pharmacist, he said, I've been robbed eighteen times, I've been shot in the heart, he said, now I'm an Alpha client and they've left me alone, I can leave the pharmacy open all night long, nobody does anything clever. And after the pharmacist, someone drove past, blew his horn, and said drop by, sure thing, I said, but I didn't even know who he was. Later, a lady took my hand and said she was happy to meet me, my name is Anne, she said, I'm Swedish. I asked what Sweden was like and she said, I don't remember, I left there when I was very young. Another woman told me her mother had died, she was very fond of you, she said. My condolences, I said. Someone asked what I thought about the government's new economic measure and I didn't have a view on it, I think it's a good one, I said. See how they love you? Gonzaga said, sitting down beside me at the table. If the Secretary for Safety was elected, everybody'd vote for you. But there's one thing, he said, the curfew, you decreed a curfew here in the neighborhood, after ten pm nobody can leave their house, that's no good, the night schools have to let the students go early, there's a lot of people unhappy, put an end to it, it's no longer necessary, we've already cut down the violence. All right, I said, put up a sign here: curfew lifted. Another thing, he said: the playground, open up the playground so the children can play soccer. I didn't remember closing down the playground. It was because they were ruining the grass, you ordered it closed. Funny, I didn't remember that. All right, I said, open the playground. You're one incredible guy, Gonzaga said, you've got a heart of gold.

I left there feeling better, the vodka brought me a sensation of peace. Heart of gold. I walked along, went into Mr Humberto's shop. Fire-eater. He hugged me tightly, you've put on weight, he said. Come and see my car. He loved my car, you're doing very well, he said. Come and have lunch with me, I said. I took Mr Humberto to the most expensive local restaurant, order shrimp, I said, shrimp was the most expensive dish, you can order it. We ordered Portuguese wine, it's expensive, but we're going to order it, I said, bring two bottles, I told the waiter. We ate and drank and then ordered dessert and coffee and liqueur. How's Dona Maria? I asked. He told me his life was still hell. He opened the top buttons of his shirt and showed me an enormous wound on his chest, she threw hot water on me.

I can take care of that for you, I said.

You can have a talk with her?

I can kill your wife, I said. In friendship.

Mr Humberto's eyes gleamed. I thought he liked the idea. You filthy son of a bitch, he said, so everything they say about you is true, you kill criminals, you kill abandoned children, killer, killer, killer, I hope lightning strikes you and splits your skull, you filthy son of a bitch.

Mr Humberto was screaming, everyone in the restaurant started looking at us, take it easy, I said. Get your monkey paws off me, he said. And he left.

Stares. They were laughing. Everybody. I went to the bathroom, sat on the toilet and stared at my shoes. I hadn't cried in a long time. I cried and left.

When I got back to the office it was late afternoon and there was an urgent message to call Santana. Everything's taken care of with Marcão, he said. Where is he? I asked. In hell, he replied.

You keep walking back and forth in the living room, you sit down, you get up, you look out the window, you turn on the television, you turn off the television, I'm like that myself, I say, tomorrow I'm going to stay by the pool sunning and that'll be nice, I go to the pool, the sun is beautiful, but it's not nice, you must be like me, Érica said. I can lay down on this satin sofa and stay on this satin sofa, there's always something, something here inside, here in my chest, something alive and rusted, I can feel that you're just like that, both of us, we prepare for happiness, a great future, but when the future gets here, we don't feel good in it. They killed Marcão, I said. Érica went pale, who killed Marcão? Santana had Marcão killed in jail.

Érica: And did you slap Santana in the face? Did you call Santana a miserable cur? Did you tell Santana he was a stinking lowlife?

Santana, a few minutes earlier, at the precinct: A son of a bitch traitor, Marcão is a traitor. And you, who are you?

You're a community leader. You have a career ahead of you. Tell me, what would you have had me do? Go on, tell me.

Érica: Tell me, Máiquel, did you tell Santana he's a stinking lowlife? So everything they say about you is true, killer, killer, killer, I hope lightning strikes you and splits your skull, in the restaurant, everybody laughing at me, Marlênio, if we turned ourselves in to the police, punch, if we felt repentance for our faults, punch, and sins, punch, we'd be saved and escape, punch, the fires of hell, OK, OK, OK, said Érica, angrily, pushing me away from her, you don't have to explain, she said, I just want to know how the two of you killed my friend Marcão. The two of you, she said.

Me: Marcão was sleeping, one of his cellmates jumped on his stomach, from the window, that's how it happened.

We went to the wake, Marcão's body in the cheap coffin, in the kitchen, the burner lit, beans in the pressure cooker, a few friends, the family, neighbors, everybody hugged me and cried and asked for favors and for vengeance.

We went home, Érica's feet on the car dashboard, all this killing, she said, and didn't complete the sentence.

We went to bed, both of us sleepless. I saw that night that Érica was thinking about leaving me. I made her promise she wouldn't leave me. I made Érica promise she'd never speak to Marlênio again.

Érica got an almanac from the nightstand, leafing through it without interest, Russian poets. The hurricane, fire, the sea is coming with fury, that's all I read, I closed my eyes. That was a warning. Evil.

28

The Santo Amaro Recreation Club has the pleasure to invite you to its Citizen of the Year ceremony, where you will be recognized for your services to the community.

I called Dr Carvalho and told him the news, how wonderful, he said, I'm very happy, we'll talk later, I have a patient in the chair.'
Congratulations, said Gonzaga.
Congratulations, said the doorman to my building.
Congratulations, said Fátima, my secretary.
This comes at a good time, said Santana, a few days ago I was talking with that friend of mine, the broadcaster, and he said, you ought to have Máiquel run for councilman.
Councilman, citizen of the year, that bubbled in my blood, my veins, my heart, it began to ache, ache from happiness, I plunged into it, simply plunged, plunged with contentment, of everything that had happened in my life nothing enthused me as much as those few lines, I survived, I won, I regained my confidence, I stopped

thinking foolish thoughts and went back to work, peacefully.

Everything under control; only one thing worried me: Érica.

I showered and as I was shaving, Érica came into the shower, she was acting very strangely, didn't say good morning, didn't give me a kiss, she always brought a cup of warm coffee, let me shave you, she'd say. She'd pick up the newspaper and sit on the bench by the sink, reading our horoscopes. But that day she didn't do any of those things, she came into the shower, everything all right? I asked, she didn't even answer. White trousers, white shirt, white shoes. I got dressed and went to show her, Érica, do you like these white shoes? No reply.

I had breakfast and left. The day was beautiful. I got my car from the garage, drove around the block and stopped at the corner, several yards from my building. I turned on the radio, five million copies sold to date in the United States alone, said the announcer, let's listen to the third cut on the LP, I changed the station, Libras, watch what you eat.

It wasn't long before Érica appeared. A tiny top, her navel showing, a full blue skirt. She got into a taxi, with me behind her. The taxi stopped at a flower stand, Érica bought daisies. Next stop, a fruit stand, apples, pears and persimmons, I love persimmons. Then, as I'd thought, Érica got out at the hospital where Marlênio was.

Flowers and persimmons, Érica walking down the corridors, looking at the room numbers, I came up behind her, caught her by the arm, let me go, she said, the persimmons fell to the floor. I shoved her into the car, she was crying, you didn't have to break Marlênio's arm, she said. Listen, Érica, I'm going to tell you who Marlênio is, Marlênio is a Jim Jones, one of those Joneses who show up on television involved in collective suicide, I read that, the Joneses are more and more powerful, they beat their followers, I even heard that Jones forced a poor woman to have sexual relations with a monkey, those guys are crazy, take a look at this newspaper clipping I brought for you, Hungary, Armenia, Biafra, Vietnam, the Joneses are everywhere, all they want is to make money, can't you see that? Érica wouldn't stop crying. I'm afraid, she said, I don't feel safe anymore, I wake up and right away think of a hecatomb, I think that the earth is going to shake, I look at the sky, I see the blue and I miss the time when I used to look at the blue sky with my father, I was worthy, now I feel dirty, life is nothing but filth and we're sunk in that filth, she said.

I took Érica home, locked her in our bedroom, you're going to spend the day locked in there to think about it, you betrayed me, you promised me you weren't going to talk to Marlênio again. Érica threw herself at me with all her strength, I'm not going to be locked up, even if it kills me, you think I'm one of those idiots who do everything you want? I pushed Érica, she fell on the floor, blood coming from her nose. Have a nice day, I said. I locked the door and left. Érica needed to learn a lesson.

Vigilantes kill five in São Paulo, said the headline. I was at a client's premises, reading the newspaper he'd just given me, the minor R S P managed to save himself by playing dead and is in hospital, out of danger, the story said. Goddamnit, I said, how did that bastard manage to get away?

That's what I wanted to ask you, my client said, I don't want any problems.

I left, dying to find Enoque. That incompetent, I'd show him a thing or two.

We left in two cars, Enoque was with me, I didn't speak to him, I simply ignored him as if I was alone in the car. How's it going to go down? he asked. Tell him that we're going to invade the emergency ward, I said. There wasn't anyone else in the car, but I got a kick out of talking like that, as if a third person was conveying my orders to Enoque. Stop it, he said, how was I supposed to know the guy wasn't dead, he had six bullets in him. Ask him what time it is, I said. Enoque paused, as if waiting for a speaker to transmit the question, then answered: eleven o'clock. Tell him that right now I ought to be drinking my whiskey and that it irritates me having to be on the street cleaning up the mess he caused, I said.

I parked my car and Hermógenes, a recent Alpha employee, immediately signaled with his lights and pulled in behind me. With him was Welton, a 6′6″ gorilla who I called on only for special operations.

We got out.

Here's how it's going to be, I said: Enoque goes in holding Hermógenes by the arm, saying he's not feeling good. Let's say he's got heart trouble.

Wouldn't it be better to go in from the rear? Enoque asked.

Tell him I make the decisions here, I said to Hermógenes. Hermógenes didn't understand why I didn't speak directly to Enoque, but he obeyed my order: he decides.

I continued: Welton and I will do the rest.

Enoque and Hermógenes went to the emergency-ward entrance, we waited in the distance. We saw the attendant come out, followed by our men. At the door, wearing motor-cycle masks to cover our faces, we forced the attendant and the security man to go with us to the ward. I'll co-operate, the security man said, you don't have to point the gun at me.

When we got to the ward the kid started yelling. Four stabs to the chest and two bullets.

I went home and slept in the guest room. Érica told me she wanted to sleep alone.

29

I've never understood why Brazil has this prejudice against
three-button coats, the tailor said. The wet bar in the living
room, imports, pistachio nuts. Want something to drink? I
asked. No, he replied, but I'll take some coffee. I dialed the
kitchen, bring a cup of coffee for my tailor. There are pins
in the coat, it's better if you don't move around too much,
he said. Lots of mirrors in my apartment's living room, I
could see the suit from every angle, front, back and side.
The first fitting is very important, the tailor said, it's when
you define the essentials, the look, the soul of a suit. In front
of the mirror, my hands in the pockets, the blazer open, I
buttoned it up. No, said the tailor, the third button of a suit
is never done up, just the top two. Of course, I said, I just
wanted to see how it looked. We're prejudiced, he said, last
summer the Europeans went crazy over checked shirts, they
were a success, but Brazilians are scared to death of checked
shirts. Cool, I thought, looking at my image in the mirror.
Another example, he said, two-tone shoes, they were a hit
in Europe and the United States, but here it's very hard to

find anyone who wears two-tone shoes. On my feet: black shoes with a golfer-type saddle. See the shoulders? asked the tailor. They were perfect. They don't look good, he said, I'm going to have to reduce them, you're short, skinny, you can't walk around with a shelf on your shoulders. Short, skinny, I don't like that. Finely cut, that's what I meant to say. You're quite elegant.

The maid came in carrying a tray of coffee, there's a man downstairs asking to speak with you, she said.

Good afternoon, my name is Max, I'm a police investigator, said the guy as soon as I opened the door.

The body, they were discovering things, Cledir, putting pieces together, Marcão, they couldn't prove anything, I thought, I was inside a Prince of Wales suit, please come in. I'd like to ask you a few questions about your wife, he said. Of course, I said, you don't mind if my tailor goes on working, do you? The Santo Amaro Recreation Club is going to honor me, a pain, I said, I have to put on a suit. Do you recognize this bracelet? Max asked. No, I answered, the cuff, I said, the tailor started marking the trouser cuff. The investigator: It was found in the backyard of Marcos Soares's house, near the spot where we found the body of a woman a few days back. The cuff's still too long, I said, what's with this cuff? I can't shorten it any further, the tailor said, it has to cover the instep.

So they found a bracelet near the body, so what? What body? Who can prove the bracelet belonged to the body? They assume the body is Cledir. They presume the bracelet belonged to Cledir. They presume I killed Cledir, so what? Suppositions, hypotheses, none of that is worth a thing, and that's why our conversation was very calm, he asked and I answered confidently, I didn't see it, I don't know anything, I wasn't there, a shame. I'm very sorry. Really very sorry.

He was about to leave, going out the same way he came in, uncertain, the tailor was leaving too, let's take the elevator together, they said, and at that moment Érica returned from the pool, entering the living room in her bikini. Max was disturbed by Érica, the red bikini, a colorful scarf tied around her hair, a gold chain on her left ankle, he stood there in the middle of the room, looking for some pretext, I'll leave you my phone number, Max said, do you have a piece of paper? I was afraid, I tried to get Érica out of there. Érica, show the tailor to the door, I said. No need, said that bastard of a tailor, I can find my own way, ciao. The three of us stood there in the living room, Érica stuck out her hand, pleased to meet you, she said, same here, he replied, Max. Here's the paper, I said.

I don't know if Érica was unaware he was a cop, maybe she was, Érica was a bag of skin ready to explode. What's Cledir's bracelet doing here? she asked.

Érica seated on our bed, in her bikini.

Listen, Máiquel, let me speak: the president of Mozambique has a terrible disease, he went to the most important doctors in the world, in France, Germany, the specialists all said the same thing, we don't know what's wrong with you, nobody could diagnose it, every day the president got worse, weaker, until he received a tape with hymns from Marlênio's church. The president started listening to the hymns, listened and began vomiting carps, live carps, live rabbits, live snakes, and he was cured. His disease was hatred, hatred is the same thing as cancer, leukemia, it kills, it eats the person away from inside, that's what I'm trying to tell you. Fuck the president of Africa, I said, you're ruining everything, Érica, you've got a beautiful apartment, you've got a car, you've got a blue swimming pool, you've got plans, flowers, money, you've got my love, but you don't think that's enough, you go around crying because of Marlênio's broken arm, Marlênio is an idiot, a Jim Jones piece of shit who keeps putting crazy ideas in your head, you saw it, that investigator left here believing that the bracelet was Cledir's, one more point for them, one less point for me, now he's going to start poking around in my life, tormenting me, and it's your fault, you listen to what that fool tells you and destroy everything, ruin everything. It's you who's ruining everything, she said, you started my heart beating, you lit a fire inside me, that's how it was at first, the world didn't exist for me, only you, only what you said, and now, look what you're doing, you're another person, can't you see what these guys are doing to you, what that suit is doing to you, what this apartment is doing to you, you've changed, you used to like going out with me, you liked to have fun, to laugh, now, now it's shit, you don't feel anything, you never turn your back, you don't sleep, and when you do sleep something inside you stays awake, baying, there's a Doberman running through your veins, broken glass in your blood, there are other things too, iron bars, walls, barbed wire, all of that is what won't let you sleep, all of that is what's killing you, eating away at you, you think I don't know what you do, you make money by killing people, and it doesn't even matter to you anymore, all of you kill those poor bastards and then go to Gonzaga's for a beer, you kill people and then go home and receive congratulations, the people are buried and rot under the ground, they leave a trail of pain and none of you even wants to know about it, all of you kill, kill without motive, kill to make money.

Shut up, Érica, I shouted. I won't shut up, you can't order me around, she said, and she opened the closet and started taking out her clothes, I'm leaving, she said, I'm tired, I love you, but alive, not as a mummy, as the poet said, you don't even know what poetry is, all you know is how to go out and kill miserable wretches. T-shirts, blouses, tank tops, shorts, everything stuffed into the suitcase, the whole thing made me sad. I kneeled at Érica's feet, don't do this to me, my love, don't leave me. Érica didn't say a word, she went on doggedly stuffing her clothes into the suitcase. I got up, went to the bathroom, washed my face. I came back to the bedroom, got my weapon, unpack that suitcase, I said. Érica went pale. You're not leaving this apartment alive, I said. And if you do leave, I'll come after you, I'll find you anywhere in the world, and kill you. I took aim at the window and fired.

30

I climbed up on the stage, my heart was like a time-bomb. Applause. I'd like to say, applause, I'd like to say that I'm very touched, applause, receiving the title of Citizen of the Year is a very great honor, I said, applause, the populace clap clap clap I'd like to thank the mayor, a good citizen, applause, the Secretary for Safety, a good citizen, applause, all the police in the area, applause, a woman in a red dress got up and began a standing ovation, applause, and everybody stood up, applauding, a storm of clapping, I had to interrupt my speech, the woman in red crossed the room, applause, approached the stage, I want to give you a present, applause, she said, applause, and opened her purse, took out a gun, they applauded, bang, bang, bang, three shots in my chest.

I woke up in terror. In the days before the awarding of the Citizen of the Year prize I couldn't sleep. I had frequent nightmares, a plane falling, with me in it, being run over by a tractor, someone grabbing me from behind, a tiny man piercing my eyes with an enormous lance. I felt like knocking on the door to Samantha's bedroom where Érica had been sleeping since our fight, screaming for help, Érica didn't even look at me anymore, refused to speak to me.

I felt an awful premonition, something was going to happen. I decided to go to a voodoo priest. He told me to tattoo a seven-pointed star on my prick, it'll hurt, he said, you'll faint from the pain, but it's necessary to seal your body.

I got the tattoo. I used Japanese mineral paint, the best in the world, and American needles, the best in the world.

Every night before going to bed I would strip, stand naked in front of the mirror, admiring the tattoo. It got to the point where I would get an erection, just so I could see the star in its most powerful form, with the seven points, each one indicating a path of the universe. Once, I saw it glow in the middle of the night. I was drunk and tired, but I'm sure of it: it glowed. And when it glowed, I prayed: seven-pointed star, take me back to a place in Érica's heart.

31

Gabriela appeared at the door to the hallway and motioned at me. I pretended not to see her.

I'll tell you what we need, Dr Carvalho said, we need a policy of paralysis gas, we need a policy of brass knuckles, a policy of knives, that's what we need. We're like the French in the sixteenth century: we want to watch the spectacle. The French loved to see scenes of execution. They liked it so much that, once, an executioner, not having a condemned person to hang, burned a sack of live cats so as not to disappoint the crowd. That's more or less what's happening now.

Gabriela reappeared at the door, ran her hands over her breasts, stuck out her tongue, the girl was halfway over the edge, that's the only thing it could be, conceited girl, if her father saw her, I was fucked.

Two councilmen sitting in front of me. Santana had organized the meeting, an informal chat, he said, let's find out what they think of us launching your candidacy for councilman.

Councilman 1, drinking coffee: The other day I saw on

television a woman who took part in a lynching and this is what she said: I don't know what happened, I was in the street, I heard shouts, I picked up a piece of wood, and by the time I realized what was going on I was already putting out the boy's eyes. Don't think she was sorry. Her expression was that of someone who'd slept well.

Councilman 2: When we kill a son of a bitch we forgive anything.

Santana: Pass the sugar, please.

Councilman 2: You ought to do what I do, Santana. Give up sugar. With artificial sweetener my belly's way down. But you're right, Carvalho, and I'll tell you something else, this shit isn't going to change. Our penal code is a joke.

Carvalho: It's fine for Switzerland.

Councilman 2: A joke. We don't punish anybody.

Santana: And when we think we have, we have to swallow the bending of the penal code. It's a bitter pill.

The telephone rang. It's for you, sir, said the maid. I took the call in Dr Carvalho's office. It was Gabriela, on the other line, come to my bedroom, I want to tell you something. I hung up the phone, went back to the living room. Well? asked one of the councilmen, does that mean you've decided to take the plunge?

They wanted me to say something. I didn't have a proposal of any kind, no speech. But I knew about things, I felt a huge desire to be useful to these people. They wanted me to play the game, and that was easy for me because I had already learned to play the game. The game goes like this: they bark and you take off. You take off and they wait for you to return, barking and drinking whiskey. Go into the woods, they say, and you go into the woods, they wait there in their car, waiting and talking about what the hotel in Miami is like. You go into the dark, you step in mud, you sink in the mud, and if you come back empty-handed they beat you. You take off, you run away, they come after you and ask if there's something you want, anything. You accept. You accept and they order you to fetch something they want. Meanwhile, they close off the porch with bars. You in the woods and them reeking of aftershave. Bars. You in the woods, you in the dark, them in the clearing, in the air conditioning. You find what they want and, again, you do what they want. And you come back, you bring a hunk of bleeding flesh, they eat, they like it. They like it and they stroke your head. And they give you a piece of sugar. No, they don't give you sugar, it's horses that like sugar, and you're not a horse. You're a dog. You're a son of a bitch dog and you don't know you're a son of a bitch dog, because that's part of the game too, not knowing. And later comes the second part of the game, which goes like this: you take a bullet in the ass and they don't pay it any heed, hey, a bullet in the ass is part of the game, they say. And when you fall down dead, they say: that's the way it is, it's part of the game.

That part of the game, the bullet in the chest, I hadn't experienced yet, all I knew how to do was bark and distribute the bloody chunks of meat. I played my part without a hitch. They were pleased. And the most important thing: I was pleased too. I was happy with myself. I thought that was just how it was, and I was willing to go on.

You should come and visit the Council Hall, they said, and I accepted.

I got into my car, Gabriela was in the back seat, totally bombed out. I want to kiss you, she said. I felt like smashing her in the face, get out, I said. Don't you have anything? she asked. Coke, crack, marijuana, anything, she said. Get out, Gabriela.

When I arrived home, the maid updated me on Érica: she woke up at ten, played with Samantha in the pool, spoke on the phone with the manicurist, watched a movie on television, slept, went to the corner to buy a comic book. Who went to the corner with her? I asked. I did, the maid said.

I thought about smoothing things over with Érica. The day of the award was close, maybe she'd agree to go with me. I gathered my courage and went ahead. Érica was in a T-shirt and panties, sleeping beside Samantha. A book was open on the bed. In it, a piece of folded paper. I opened it. Érica's handwriting. There were lots of drawn circles, arrows connecting the circles, she always drew that design. Beside it was written: birth and death, fucking and death, betrayal and death, escape and death, work and death, creation and death, screaming and death, planting and death, striving and death, aging and death, cure and death, study and death, victory and death, loss and death, love and death.

I gave up on smoothing things over. Érica was too much of a goddamn drag.

32

E noque and me at the office.

The guys are right, Enoque said. Seven tape players stolen on Comércio Street alone, they're mad as shit, and with good reason, it looks like we're here sitting on our hands, that's what they think, we pay you, they say, we pay to have peace and we don't have peace. And they also stole the baker's television set.

My anger was long since gone, but I continued to speak to Enoque through an invisible third party, just to irritate him.

Ask him who's doing it, I said.

Those little shits who work with Duke, he answered. Duke is cool, he respects our agreement. Duke, let me tell you, Duke is one really cool dealer, a guy with character. A high-class type. He doesn't invade our turf. The problem is those little shits, they steal our tape players, our sneakers, our watches, our gold hearts, and take them to Duke to trade for coke and crack. Except Duke doesn't know they're stealing in our area because the little shits go there and say they stole from somewhere else. There's another issue: Duke has to control his personnel. It's his fucking responsibility. He made a deal, and a deal is a deal.

Ask him if Duke has been informed of what's happening.

No, Enoque said.

Tell him his shoelace is untied, I said.

Enoque tied his shoelace.

Tell him he can go, I said.

I picked up the phone and called Duke.

Enoque, on his way out, stopped at the door, a serious expression on his face, respectful, looked at me and said: Tell him I said bye.

The planes fly so low here, Duke said, that you can read what's written on their fuselage.

We were in Duke's shack, in the Vietnam shantytown. He waited for another plane to go by and then continued: The noise gets in your blood and shakes around inside you, and after it's gone you're still shaking like a blender. I'm used to it, but there's guys who come here and flip out.

Duke laid out two enormous lines, there's no boric acid in this stuff, he said, no marble dust, you can snort it.

I snorted. Great stuff. Coke, when it's good, has the same effect as eyeglasses on a near-sighted person. It corrects the world.

I don't know if you remember, Duke said, that Boeing belonging to an Israeli company that crashed into a couple of apartment buildings in Holland. The pilot's last words recorded on the black box were: I'm falling. Whaddya think? I live here with these planes blowing my hair around, I remember that story every day, every damned day I remember that story, I'm falling, I'm falling, isn't that shit? I dream about that black box, whaddya think? Can you picture anything that horrible, to be falling and know you're falling? Can you picture the desperation? There was another plane, from China, that hit a mountain. The engines caught fire right after take-off. The pilot saw that mass of earth approaching, can you picture it? The guy saw death coming toward him at five hundred miles an hour, whaddya think? Strong stuff, huh? You couldn't fucking pay me to get on an airplane. And it isn't fear of flying, either. It's fear of falling. Of falling in the sea and being eaten by sharks. If they could guarantee the plane would fall on land, I'd fly. But the problem is that here in Brazil there's lots of rivers, lots of water, lots of ocean. That's my problem, everybody's got something blocking their path. I'm always going to be a ten-kilo dealer, that's my ceiling, ten kilos, a middle-level dealer, because I wouldn't get in an airplane even if it was to bring back the crown jewels. I had the chance to work for that guy who was arrested with a truckload of cocaine, you remember him? But I would've had to go by plane. You had to go to Bolivia by plane, just picture it, falling in some river in the jungle, whaddya think? Rivers in the jungle have piranhas, you ever see a cow being eaten by piranhas? I turned him down. I'd rather stay here with my nice little ten kilos. It's very good, did you like the coke?

A gigantic black guy came in hauling a skinny kid, shabbily dressed, fifteen at most. The television set's already in the car, said the giant.

Let's go, said Duke.

We all went to Duke's car, the kid, the television set, and the giant in the back seat. On the way, Duke continued to talk about plane crashes. Human error, they say. Technical error, I don't even want to know, those contraptions are all the time falling on top of us.

We arrived at the bakery, got out, the kid in great distress. Yes, that's it, said the baker as soon as he saw the television. He wants to apologize, Duke said. I'm sorry, the boy said. What else? Duke asked. I'm not going to do that anymore, the boy said. Very good, everything's all right then, I said.

As we were getting into the car, the baker called us back. Can I ask a favor? Sure, Duke said. I'd like to punch that idiot who stole my television in the face. The kid had already got into the car. C'mere, kid. Go ahead, Duke said. The baker spit in the palm of his hand and hit the kid in the face with full force, smack, the boy stood his ground. We left. In the car, Duke saw the boy wanted to cry. If you cry, Duke said, if you cry I swear I'll cornhole you. I swear to God.

33

Érica had refused to go to the Citizen of the Year ceremony with me even though I'd given her a long golden dress. You can ask any policeman, she said, the ones who train dogs, tell them I have a puppy that's an idiot, it doesn't bark, it doesn't bite, what should I do? Well, they'll say, put that useless puppy in a pack and immediately you'll have a lion on your hands. Yes, in the pack, the pack is shit heading together, and growing, and breaking glass, and beating up its adversaries, and smashing shop windows, and looting, and raping. That's what happened with you, she said, and that's why you're getting a medal. They're proud because they taught you that, hatred, the mud, and you love that hatred and that mud, all that filth, you love it, love it like a scared puppy loves the pack, that mud, and do you know why? Not because you're a lion, far from it. It's because through hatred you feel equal to those guys who'll be there at the dance and have done well in life by fixing broken things, selling, renting, planting, building, operating, buying, stealing, administrating, lying, and hiring you, and that's why you're getting a medal, she said.

I slapped Érica in the face. Fine, she said, that's the last straw, you've done the only thing that was missing between us, she said, and I left Érica standing in the middle of the living room, turned my back and went to the party.

The valet opened the car door for me, I got out, Prince of Wales, my Italian shoes on the sidewalk, heading for the entrance to the Recreation Club, click, click, click, a beggar on the ground, my shoes, all he saw was my shoes, raising his head was impossible for the poor devil, my brand-new Italian shoes, shiny, the face in the asphalt, click, click, click, good evening, rich man, the beggar said. Get that man out of here, the doorman shouted. Rich man, the beggar was right, it began from the feet up, it was there more than any other part of my body that I felt rich.

Come over here, Máiquel, Santana said, I'd like to introduce you to the judge. The attorney. The doctor. The councilman. The civil servant. The pediatrician. The businessman. Virginia. Blue eyes and wonderful legs. Smashing girl, that Virginia. Teaches physical education, twenty-four years old.

On the stage, the Mac Rainbow band. They're sensational, said Virginia, they only play music from the Sixties. Virginia sat down at my table and danced with me and said she didn't have a boyfriend and that I was a cool guy.

And then there was the dinner, and it was a wonderful dinner, by candlelight. In every detail, the frozen margaritas, the napkins, the politeness of the waiter, Virginia's stories, Érica didn't know anything. In every detail, I was part of all that, all of it, I was there, I belonged to it, and for that reason and no other I felt myself deserving of that medal. Because I was supposed to be outside, in the rain. More ice, I said. But I was here inside. The first course, hot; I ordered. I was supposed to be down there, in the cold. And I was on top. At the heights. On the rocks, I told the waiter. I drank all night, and I noticed something interesting: I was laughing just like those guys, laughing at the right time, I had learned that too, how to laugh with a whiskey glass in my hand.

And finally the moment for the award. There was a time when I thought a check-book and women were the basis of happiness. I climbed onto the stage. Money helps, a woman makes things a lot better, but it's fame that reinvents a man's life, that's what they taught me that night. They applauded me. They hugged me. They photographed me. They asked me to speak. I said I was thinking of running for councilman. They were very pleased. The medal, what a pretty thing a medal is.

You were great, Santana said when I returned to the table.

At the end of the evening I gave Virginia a ride home. I parked the car and we stood there talking in front of her gate. The dog wouldn't stop barking, down, she said, his name is Kiko, but at home nobody likes him, it's like that joke, we're all the time saying, down, Kiko, and now he thinks his name is Downkiko, he only obeys if you say Downkiko. Downkiko, I said, and he came running to lick my hand. Do you live with your family? she asked. I said I lived with my sister Érica. I said I wasn't married, I didn't have a girlfriend, nothing. I'm all by myself, I said. And there was a moment when we were so close that I thought a kiss would come of it, but she backed away and said she had to go inside. A decent woman. I asked for her phone number, said I'd call her the next day.

I got home and tiptoed to my room. There was an envelope on my bed. I opened it. It was a letter from Érica.

I never want to see you again, you fool. Not even if hell freezes over.

Marlênio has found a place for me, far away from here, a safe place. Don't look for me because you won't find me.

I've taken Samantha because she's my daughter and because you don't care the least thing about her.

I've taken twenty thousand dollars from the safe, I'm sorry, but I had to do it. You don't have a maid anymore, she's gone with me. The number of the agency is 322–4432, ask for Dona Márcia, she'll get you another one.

Until forever.

Érica

PS One more thing, you fool, I never did and never will go to bed with Marlênio. I still love you, but I swear I'm going to find somebody really great to love. I really am. And I'm going to be a happy girl, you'll see. As for you, I hope you get fucked, that's what I hope. I want your life to turn to shit, a living hell, and for you never to be able to forget me, and that every woman in your life is stupid, that's what you deserve, you imbecile.

I ran to Samantha's room; the beds were made. My legs felt like ice, the blood rushed to my head, boiling. I ran to Marlênio's house. Nobody. I ran to Marlênio's church. Nothing. I returned home, I called Santana, crying, that son of a bitch kidnaped my daughter, I said. Stay calm, son, I can't understand a thing. Explain to me what's going on, he said.

178

34

D on't open your eyes till I tell you to. I kept my eyes shut. I could smell the sweet perfume coming from Érica; she moved quickly through the living room, she must be wearing high heels. She fiddled with the stereo, soft music, American, the kind they play all the time on the radio, you can open your eyes now, she said. I opened them. Well, how do you like it? Érica was wearing a long gold-colored dress, her hair down, rings, lots of rings. Too much, I said. Let's dance. We danced. The telephone started ringing. Answer it, she said. Let it ring, I said. Get it, it may be something important, Érica insisted.

I woke up, the phone ringing, me on the living-room rug, a bottle of whiskey beside me. Hello?

Who is Marlênio Silvano? asked Santana at the other end of the line. The question jolted me awake and also woke up the thing that, with the help of a lot of alcohol, I had managed to put to sleep a few hours earlier, the pain, it all came back, all the shit, it hurts a lot to be abandoned, it makes you want to run off in a straight line and go around the world like that, running, never stop running, run till your heart explodes. Marlênio is a pastor, I said. I know he's a pastor, but where did the guy come from? What's he got to do with you? Nothing, I said. Nothing, shit, it can't be, the guy screwed up your life, you're messed up, Santana said, really messed up. Zé Pedro, the investigator at the 16th, just called me. I'd asked him to talk to the guy in Kidnap, I explained your case to him, I said that Érica had run off with your daughter, he asked me to hold off, and he called back to say that you're fucked, he mentioned that Marlênio guy, Marlênio went to the precinct yesterday, his arm was broken, he'd gotten out of hospital yesterday and went to the precinct to fuck you over, he said that the corpse they discovered at Marcão's house was your wife Cledir, hello, Máiquel, are you there? I'm here, I said. Marlênio said you killed Cledir by strangling her, hello, Máiquel? Hello, I answered. Now those faggots in Forensics, who pissed away all that time without coming to any conclusion, are saying in unison that the body is Cledir's and that Marlênio's statement verifies everything, hello, Máiquel, did you hear what I said? I heard, I said. Did you beat up Marlênio? Yes, I answered. He also lodged a complaint against you for bodily assault, Santana replied. And he made another serious charge, that you're making death threats against Érica. The whole thing stinks, they've issued a warrant for your arrest, hello, Máiquel, do you hear me? Come down here immediately, you hear what I said?

I hung up the phone. Fear is a funny thing. It caves in your chest, swells your belly, and without realizing it, everything good starts leaking away. At least that's how it happened with me.

★ ★ ★

Gabriela opened the door. She was crazy to score some cocaine, at least that's what was written all over her. I should have gone straight to find Santana, then at least I wouldn't have had to see Gabriela's face, but I had to talk to Dr Carvalho. To ask for help. He'd help me, I knew that. Is your father here? I asked.

Máiquel, she said, my father, the asshole wants to send me away, did you know he wants to send me away? No, I said. All because my math teacher, who's a slut, just because she says I can't do long division anymore, that bitch thinks that's important, long division, I hate the woman, she's a whore, whores like her, you know, they're always fucking around with somebody's life, she went and told my father that I'm forgetting how to write, and because of that my father wants to send me to a clinic. Don't you think it's awful to be in a detox center? I wonder if they even have television in a detox center. Probably not, right? I don't even think they've got a phone in that shithole. All they've got is hysterical nurses, a friend told me that. My friend, poor woman, was in for five months, working with a hoe, digging, cooking, therapy, God help me, just thinking about cooking makes me want to slash my jugular. And what about therapy? That drag, would you like to talk about that? they ask you, in that throw-their-weight-around voice of theirs. Would you like to talk about your mother? Shall we discuss that a little? Jesus, those shrinks bore you to death. Five months, can you imagine? Discussing my relation to this, that and the other, I think I'll have to kill myself. And clinics don't do any good, they stick you there, you stop snorting, then you get out and start snorting again, I'm telling you right now, that's how it's going to be with me, 'cause I can't make it without coke. Could you help me, could you hide me at your place till my father changes his mind? It won't work, I said. And coke, could you get me a little? I don't have any, I answered. Selling coke in those places, at clinics, brings in money like crazy, she said. I can work with you, you set it up and I'll deal, we'll really score. I want to talk to your father, excuse me, Gabriela. You got any coke for me? I'm your friend. Just a little snort, you know, I'm kinda down, can't you see I'm down?

I didn't give a shit about Gabriela, in fact I wanted Dr Carvalho to send that cokehead away. I pulled her hands off me and went inside. You son of a bitch, she said, you disgusting rat. Fuck you, I thought. There's a lot of disgusting rats running around.

I found Dr Carvalho in his office, reading the paper. Guess, he said, take a guess, how much do you think the GDP has grown? I didn't have the faintest idea what he was talking about. I don't know, I said. Take a guess, go on, pick a number. I didn't take a chance, I never took chances on anything, in any situation, that was always my basic tactic. When in doubt, a friend of mine, I mean, I don't even know if he was a friend of mine, when in doubt, he used to say, remain in doubt. Five point seventy-seven, Dr Carvalho said. Take the insurance sector, do you know how much the insurance sector has grown? No, I said. Sixty-three percent, he said. You think that's possible?

It said in the newspaper that it had happened, but Dr Carvalho thought it impossible, he was very irritated about it, he ranted, spoke badly of the country, of the journalist, the newspaper, the police, and with me in such a hurry. Dr Carvalho, I said. He didn't hear, I don't even know why I read this rag of a newspaper every day, he said, I really don't, all it does is make me upset, that's what newspapers are for, he said, newspapers refresh our hatred; if your hatred is a bit on the anemic side, all you have to do is take a look at the paper, that's the truth.

Pause. He stared at me. I cleared my throat. What brings you here? he asked. I had the impression that it was only then that he realized that the person who'd come into his office and who he'd asked a bunch of idiotic questions was me.

Well, I said, and that was all I said, because Gabriela opened the office door, came in, knocked over the telephone table, fell onto the telephone table, hi, father, she said. It was enough to make me feel sorry for Gabriela.

Father, did you tell him I'm being sent away?

It was enough to make me feel sorry for Dr Carvalho too, the cripple.

I'm being sent away, Gabriela said, looking at me. I'm a cokehead. I also smoke crack, drink beer, cuba libres, whiskey, perfume, I shoot up marijuana, hash, anything. My father's going to send me away. It's a clinic outside São Paulo, a very good clinic. I'm going to get well, I'm going back to my studies, I'm going to find a fiancé, study psychology and get married and have three kids who don't snort coke. The clinic's going to help me, isn't it, father? Even to find a fiancé.

Silence. I thought about leaving the room, but the atmosphere was so heavy that any movement would have broken something very important, maybe the roof, that was my impression.

Father, I want you to know that the guy sitting in front of you, that piece of crap, who wears pleated slacks and a gold chain these days, that obscene little man who kills homeless children, sells me drugs. He was the one who got me hooked. At first he gave me coke as a gift. Later, he started charging. He's the one who won't let me stop snorting, just today he showed up and tried to sell me five grams. The guy is a filthy dog. You should take the gun out of your desk and put three bullets in his head.

Gabriela left the office, and Dr Carvalho and I sat there with that hot potato between us.

I don't sell coke, I said. He stared at me, both hands on his waist. Really, I don't sell it. Dr Carvalho stood up. I don't like such things, drugs, I said. Dr Carvalho sat down and I said three more times that I didn't sell coke. He stood up. He went to the door. Came back. Picked up the telephone. Put down the telephone. And then, without me expecting it, he picked up a paperweight on top of his prescription book and threw it at me. He hit me in the mouth, you broke my tooth, I said, you broke my tooth.

I didn't mean to, he answered, and that surprised me even more, his reply, didn't mean to. I'm sorry, he said, but I suddenly felt an insane desire to yank every tooth out of your head. You didn't hear, he said, what my daughter had to say. My daughter, he said, isn't going to be sent away. My family, he said, my family, and he didn't say anything else, he collapsed, sobbing. Then I understood. The problem wasn't me having sold coke to his daughter. The problem wasn't the fact that his daughter was a cokehead. The problem was his daughter telling me she was going to be sent away, that was what he couldn't take, people knowing. Snorting coke, fine. Taking it in the ass, fine. Stealing from your partner, killing children, fine. The problem, guys like him always think like that, is when the pipes break. The dirty water that pours out. What will the neighbors think? Guys like him live for the neighbors. They buy a new car to humiliate the next-door neighbor. They take a trip to Europe to humiliate their neighbor. It took me a long time to get their number.

I sat down beside him, Dr Carvalho, it'll be good for your daughter, the clinic, you'll see, later, nobody needs to know about it, you can say she went to Miami, to Disneyland, girls really like Disneyland, you make up a story, how would anybody know she's in the clinic? He stood up, get out, he said, you mangy dog. I left the office, a handkerchief at my mouth to hold back all that blood, with Dr Carvalho behind me, limping and cursing me for a mangy dog, a son of a bitch cur, and other such names.

I should have gone to meet Santana, he was waiting for me, but instead I drove around, my tooth broken, my gum bleeding. I stopped in a bar, asked for ice, it helped a little.

I went downtown. Then to Lapa. The Pinheiros loop. I drove all afternoon, one thing wouldn't get out of my head: piece of crap. Who wears pleated pants these days?

The night before I'd received a medal for services to the community. It wasn't yet three pm and they'd already changed their minds. Piece of crap. What kind of people were they? Just what did they want?

I stopped by Enoque's house, we went drinking.

Getting plastered was the only good thing about that wretched day. Little by little I started feeling better and forgetting that Érica had deserted me. And that Marlênio had handed me over to the cops. And that I'd been called a piece of crap. And after drinking a bit more I started calling them little pieces of crap. The guys who were there, who I didn't even know, except for Enoque, had fun with me. They laughed a lot. I also laughed like crazy.

And then, after drinking all my body would allow, I got into my car and started driving again.

The worst thing of the night was still to happen.

★   ★   ★

When I was little, in Robinson's mother's parlor there was a statue of an elephant with a tiger on its back. I thought the elephant was useless, a pile of blubber that wasn't good for anything. And the tiger, hunger, rage, impressive, I admired that hunger. I would look at those animals for hours, and it was like being at ringside waiting for the boxers who never come, never fight, never win and never lose. One day I threw the statue on the floor, I couldn't stand waiting any longer. It broke in such a way that my aunt managed to glue it back together. The elephant part, being larger, was the most damaged. The tiger was intact, victorious. The elephant, glued together, looked like a sick elephant. Destiny.

That night, driving through those dark streets, I remembered the statue, not the broken one, the original. I remembered the elephant, I felt real goddamned hatred to think that I'd once felt sorry for the elephant. The tiger was another story. In the trunk, a 7.65mm pistol and a 12-gauge shotgun. Fuck the elephant.

The tiger works in circles, circling the herd. The useless ones, those are the worst. They have nothing to do with us, the useless ones. They transform themselves into that rotten mass, the herd. They grow, they stink, they suffocate us. At the traffic light, there he was, the elephant on a skateboard. Fatty matter. A noxious thing for society. I shot. The elephant fell. I took a piece of paper from the glove compartment and wrote in his own blood: Long live the future!

Two blocks further on, I picked up a whore. Her name was Helô. Helô, I said, let's go to your place. Helô was real cool and did everything I asked.

35

There was a lot of whiskey in my blood and blood on my shirt. I had just woken up, it was three in the afternoon. I sat up in bed, my head was throbbing, where was I? The smell of come on the sheets. Lots of photos stuck on the wall. Helô, I recognized Helô, she was dressed like a Bahian woman. Helô's place, how nice. Helô, I shouted.

From somewhere outside came the sounds of a pressure cooker, a child's voice. I closed my eyes, tried to sleep, but couldn't. Very hot. Helô, I shouted again.

Helô came into the bedroom holding a newspaper. It's a good thing you're awake. Take a look at this: isn't this guy you? she asked.

Long live the future was the headline. A photo of the kid I'd killed, one of him on a skateboard. Blue sneakers, a Hang Ten shirt. His knees were bent, he was holding a guitar, I mean, he was posing, there wasn't any guitar. High-school sophomore, boyfriend of Isabela, fifteen years old, a good son, a good grandson, a good friend, a good neighbor, a good student.

The article said the boy had been murdered in the early hours the night before as he was returning home. Father: pediatrician. Mother: owner of a boutique. An only child. Brutally murdered, six shots. The note, the terrible, vile note had left the populace outraged. The Secretary for Safety promised justice. The assassin had left a priceless clue: the note had been written on an Alpha business card. My name, address and telephone number. My God, how could I have done that? Below, my photo: the killer. Someone had jotted down the license plate of my car. My background: he killed his wife, buried the woman, and so on and so forth. Owner of a murder for hire agency. Wanted by the police. Police beginning to investigate other crimes.

Is it all true what they say there? Helô asked. Of course not, I replied. Can I take a shower?

The shower was outside the house, I had to say hello to a bunch of women to get there, two old women, lots of boys also, a whole day-care center. My family, Helô said. My mother liked the present you gave her last night. I didn't remember giving anybody anything. I hated that, not remembering things.

I took a shower. Why, Érica, why didn't you take me with you? Father: pediatrician. How was I to know? How was I to know the kid was a good student? At night, on a skateboard, he looked like a thief in Reeboks. How was I to know? It was a mistake. I admit I made an error. I killed somebody by mistake. Look, people are constantly screwing up. People make mistakes at times. Doctors make mistakes, they make mistakes in dosage, they amputate healthy legs, they pierce intestines, they cause hemorrhages. And other things too, bus drivers who fall asleep at the wheel, prosecutors, judges, legal mistakes. How was I to know?

You don't have the face of a killer, Helô said, I know killers, just by looking at his face I know if the guy's a killer. You recognize a killer by his eyes, you know? Killers have birds' eyes, she said. Helô, I said, can I ask a favor?

Whores love doing favors. Helô rented a car for me. I waited for her at the corner. She got out of the car, I love to drive, don't you want me to drive for you? No, I said. I gave her some dough, mum's the word, I said. Don't be a stranger, she said as I was leaving.

By the end of the afternoon I was arriving at Santana's country home.

I broke in the rear door and entered. I called Santana at the precinct. You son of a bitch, he said, where the hell are you?

36

You killed somebody you shouldn't have, Santana said, and you know what that means? It means you put a bullet in your own head.

When Robinson died, when they told me he had died, Robinson, something crazy went through my head, I knew that he was dead, but I thought that if somebody did something, he could live, we could put the death right.

A shot in the head, OK, we can fix that. It was a mistake, I admit it, I said. Admit it, you admit it, Santana screamed, what's this admit it business? It was suicide, Santana said, if you want to admit something, admit you committed suicide.

I didn't want to hear anymore, I hung up the telephone. I hadn't told Santana where I was. He never went to the country house because his wife only liked the beach, I don't like grazing, she often said. I decided I'd stay there for a time. It was either stay there or risk being arrested. There was no way I would go back and get arrested. I never thought that could happen to me, getting arrested. You expect anything, the worst, you prepare for whatever comes, but being arrested, never. Cancer. Dying in a gun battle, yes, we can accept a gun battle, but not being arrested. Cirrhosis, getting run over, we can accept that. Getting knifed in the back, revenge, a bad guy catching you by surprise, fine, we can face that, but being arrested, no. No and no. Things would straighten themselves out, I thought. There was no way I was going to jail.

I wasn't too far from understanding that there's over here and over there, and nobody changes sides. Never. You can think you've changed, they make you think so, come in and close the door, they say, you go in, you think you're over there, you close the door, you think you've changed, but no, in reality it's not a change, if you're over there it's because they need somebody to wash their marble lavatory. It's that simple.

Anyway, I hadn't understood that yet, I was very confused, I still thought I was over there, something was pushing me toward here, them, but I had to resist, push, over there, strength, reconciliation, that was what I wanted, to return to my home, there, with them, that was pushing me toward here.

I felt a kind of hatred for being hated by them, pushing me, but it wasn't true hatred, I pretended I hated, I went on admiring all of that, their little world, I wanted to be there, to be part of it, I had won their hearts, I soothed their ulcer, as Dr Carvalho once said; now, he said, that you're in action, we can sleep better. I could go back to doing that, taking action.

I only left the house very early in the morning to buy newspapers, and the papers made me desperate. I was in the news every day, my picture in the newspaper, always the same picture, the one as Citizen of the Year, me going into the Recreation Club. Everyone had something to say about me. Killer. Vigilante. Murder for hire, they, the journalists, loved to write that, murder for hire. Idiots, journalists are idiots. Amnesty International, the Commission for Peace and Justice, always the same guys saying the same thing. The fruit of authoritarianism, they said. Of impunity. Of the abuse of power. The only thing that enraged me was the president of the Recreation Club, we could never have imagined that he would do such a thing, he said, awarding that fellow a medal was a mistake. Asshole. I did feel anger toward that asshole. Why say it was a mistake? Couldn't he at least have kept his mouth shut, the asshole?

And what about the teacher, Virginia? I thought about her. She liked me. She was impressed by me, the medal. I had said I'd phone her. It might be a good thing. I decided to call her. She didn't even try to hide it, tell him I'm not in, she said, right near the mouthpiece, I heard everything. She's not in, the maid said. One less. Little by little, they were all abandoning me.

The days passed, with me waiting for things to get better, but things got worse. They started talking about Santana. I had friends in the police, the headline said. The statement was made by an investigator. He said I played soccer with a group of police, every week. It was true. The article also said I used an official car to carry out the executions. True. That Santana was a partner in Alpha. True. Santana denied everything. I know the perpetrator, he said, but we never had business dealings. I didn't like that, perpetrator, what was that about him calling me a perpetrator? It was his girlies who were perpetrators. The investigator also said that when I wrecked my car I circulated a donation list among the residents and merchants in my neighborhood. An outright lie. I never wrecked my car, I had it painted, the merchants paid, that part, OK, it was true.

After those accusations I stopped reading the papers. I still bought them, but I stacked them in the living room. It was better not to know about anything.

The days, my God, the days seemed to be stuck together with screws, they wouldn't end. I felt an awful sadness, I should have picked some other place to run away to, every time I go to the countryside I feel like killing myself. The sky can be blue and the glory bushes loaded with flowers, nothing changes my mood. The cows, the cows' gaze makes me sad. I could have gone to the coast, the waves, the women, the sea is better. The countryside is a lie. You look out the window and there's all that goodness on a silver platter, humans offering cornbread to strangers, I don't know, I don't believe it. Man isn't good. I only felt that kind of consolation when I got plastered. Or when I slept. I dreamed about Érica. About Samantha too. I developed a special technique for dreaming about them. I repeated their names for over three hours, without stopping even for a second. It worked. One night I dreamed that Érica, Samantha and I were on a boat, we were going to the Caribbean. Holiday. Another night, I dreamed that Érica telephoned me, I want to come back, she said, I love you, she said. Come back, I answered. That was when I woke up, alone.

Watching television and taking baths was all I had to do. Or walk around the house, talking to myself, Érica, Érica, Érica.

One day I couldn't take it anymore and I called Alpha, any word from Érica? I asked. The phone is tapped, Fátima said. I hung up. Good old Fátima.

I have no idea how many days went by, a week, maybe.

One night I woke up to the sound of a car. I froze. My gun was on the dresser, but I couldn't even reach out my arm to get it. I hid under the bed, that was all I could manage to do.

Someone in the living room. Sounds on the stairs. Suddenly, the bedroom light came on. The boots, I recognized Santana's boots. Máiquel, he said, we have to talk.

There I was under the bed.

My neighbor, he said, my neighbor phoned saying there was a man in my house. Lucky for you, he said, that he didn't call the police.

I came out from under the bed. That wasn't cool. A man, I don't know, a man wouldn't do that. I did it. My T-shirt was all dirty from the dust. I wiped it off.

Your situation, he said, your situation is very serious. Extremely serious, I'd say. You've stirred up the human-rights activists, the bishops, the cardinals, that bunch, I'm going to tell you something, that bunch is heavy-duty, they make one hell of a stink. The Secretary for Safety is so mad he's foaming at the mouth. I can just imagine the flak the poor guy caught from the governor. Why? Because the governor, man, if he could, he'd bring you in with his own hands. Normally he wouldn't give a shit about you. He'd even consider you a good thing, you're useful, he might even think like that. But it happens that the Minister of Justice, because of the bishops, the cardinals, all that carnival in the newspapers, he's no fool, the minister, he decided to capitalize on this shitty situation and promised to put the Federal Police on the case. Well, that's where you screwed up royally. You're between a rock and a hard place, you know how it is? The governor felt humiliated, understand? He thought the minister was trying to make him the patsy, you know how it is, those guys enjoy playing each other for suckers. A rock and a hard place. So the governor said he didn't need anybody's help. That he'll catch you if he has to go to the gates of hell to do it, that was the expression he used, to the gates of hell, Zé Pedro told me, the head detective told Almir, who's a friend of Zé Pedro's. Almir is a fire-eater. Which means, the thing came rolling down from up there, from the minister, and fell on top of us. You can't imagine, the guys are turning everything upside down. There are always ten uniforms around Alpha. As for your building, man, you can't imagine the number of cops waiting for you there. The thing's turned into something else, it's no longer a question of the fuck-up that you committed, the murdered kid, they don't care about the boy. What they want is to skin you alive. The governor wants to show off the billions his administration has spent, the new vehicles, school patrols, that kind of stuff. He wants to throw all that in the minister's face, get it? He wants to catch you, get it? That's the story.

What if I talked to him? I asked. To who? Santana replied. I don't know, those guys, the governor.

Santana roared with laughter. You can imagine how desperate I was. I laughed too, out of duty, only because he was laughing.

And when we stopped laughing, we turned serious, Santana more than me. Really serious.

I'm going to make you a proposition, he said. A really good deal for you. I think it's the only way out. You give yourself up, there'll be a big splash, then I'll find a way to get you out of there. I'm not a criminal, I said. Of course you're not. It's just till things settle down. We'll calm the secretary down, the governor, the minister, soon they'll forget about it, once you're arrested the fire will go out. They'll go after some other idiot. Idiot, that was the word he used. Idiot in this sense, Santana said, a person they can use to promote themselves, that's what I mean. I'm trying to get your ass out of this, Santana said. I can still do something for you. You're going to be arrested whatever happens. You can be arrested by me, with a deal, or you can find some wild-ass detective in your face, looking for promotion, and I'd like to see what'd happen then. So, he asked me, which do you prefer?

37

You know, she said, I have a theory. When a woman starts exercising every day, mark my words, she's putting out for some guy. Fitness centers make their money from adulteresses. Young women go surfing, or they go bicycling. Adulteresses go to fitness centers. Those who say they enjoy exercising are bald-faced liars. Exercise is one big bore, three sets of sit-ups, my God, even praying isn't as boring. So, Máiquel, if I stop exercising, first: it means I no longer enjoy going to bed with you. Second, if after a time I go back to exercising, you can beat the shit out of me. I mean it.

Give me your hand, Érica said. These muscles here, the sartorius muscles, are the ones that give me the most trouble. Hard, aren't they? They were. My hands went up a little, the panties, I pulled them off. The down close to the groin. I licked it. I had a friend who always said this: What's good is licking a pussy.

Érica had come back to our house. In the dream, of course. My dream technique had evolved a lot, actually they weren't dreams, they were my mind, I would close my eyes and enter them, so focused, so thirsty, so nostalgic, I entered them so deeply that it was as if I was dreaming. The result was I came to have a double life. One with Érica, when I slept. And another, when I woke up in prison.

Prison. If you have money, prison life is crap. If you don't have money, it's total crap, that's the difference. You have to spend a lot of money just to eat a custard pudding. But in prison a custard pudding is basic. Sometimes it's the only reason you have for not dying. But with cigarettes you can get almost anything, sex, crack, roast chicken, anything. For a pack you can buy a piece of steak. Or four eggs. Or two rolls of toilet paper. If you want to make a phone call, it's three packs. Renting a television, black and white, for one day, costs six packs. You can even get a facial, and there's a guy who does it. Twenty-four packs. For forty packs you can get a female impersonator. That I didn't need, I had Érica, thank God. In dreams. At least that.

I stayed in a special cell. The inmates hate killers, Santana said. It wasn't that. In prison, you don't have much to do. So you start looking around for something to hate. Anything, even a piece of tin will do. Because it's hate that makes you dead tired and only then can you sleep, dead. And it's also hate that gets you up the next morning, you only get out of bed if there's the possibility of hating something or someone or yourself, for lack of anything better. They chose me, the inmates. I couldn't get any sun at the same time as them. I couldn't look at them. Or say a word. But that was OK. There, in a way, I felt protected. My fear was that I'd be transferred to some other prison, but, according to Santana, that wouldn't happen for a long time, the prisons were overcrowded. Before that could happen, as we had agreed, I'd be out of there. Soon, soon.

The day I was arrested, a dozen lawyers came to speak to me. They'd been sent by Alpha clients. You know, they said, you can count on me. Do you need money? Take some money. A transistor radio? Take this transistor radio. A mirror to hang on the wall? Do you like mirrors? A better mattress? A bedspread for the mattress? Pillows to go with the bedspread? My cell filled up with comforts, a TV, fruit, tape recorder, even a vase of flowers. My cellmates liked it. In fact, that was why they left me alone, they took all my things for themselves. I didn't want any trouble, so everything was cool. In exchange, the lawyers wanted me to forget about their clients, you know, they said, we're worried, you know how it is, the questioning, they're going to want to know about other, the other, how can I put it? Crimes, was the word. But the lawyers didn't say that, crimes. Neither did I. We were full of unspoken words. It took me a long time to get rid of that foolishness. The fact is that the lawyers were scared to death I'd open my mouth, but I had no intention of opening my mouth. I just wanted out of there, that's all.

I was taken in on a Friday. On Saturday all the newspapers announced my arrest. On Sunday, three hundred residents of my neighborhood surrounded the police station demanding my release. I don't know what the repercussion of that was on the outside, I didn't read the newspapers anymore. But on the inside it caused a real stir. In my cell, the guys couldn't stop saying wow, wow, they went on saying wow for three days.

Letters arrived by the pile. Things like this: Now that you're no longer here, those lowlife pieces of scum walk past my bar twirling revolvers in their hands. Another: Release this saintly man, he does nothing but good for people. Another: Your imprisonment is a dirty deal, you're a necessary evil. The idiot, he can shove necessary evil up his ass.

Most of the time I stayed calm. But if I caught a glimpse of the sky, or heard any sound, like the mango vendors, the ones who drive minivans, I would go crazy. Nothing makes a prisoner more delirious than that, to imagine the people out there, buying mangoes.

Sometimes I spoke with Santana.

Our problem, Santana said, our problem is that we don't have bullfights, or at least something like bullfights. So they're always grabbing somebody to clobber. And it has nothing to do with morality or justice, it has to do with sports, clobbering. We don't have bullfights, that must be why. We have to clobber. They got you, that was rough, and if I slip up they'll get me too. But they'll forget you. Pretty soon they'll forget you. Remember that boy who killed his entire family? There you go, they don't remember anymore. They don't remember because some other boy who killed his entire family plus his grandparents made them forget the boy who only killed his entire family. They'll forget him too. The maid who put Ajax and urine in the food of the couple she worked for wiped him out of their memory. And now you've made them forget the maid. Soon somebody will come along to save your skin. It's that way, the domino effect, one piece knocking down the next. You may get lucky, there may come along some nut with a stiletto, some rapist of young girls, that'd be very good. Because what they need is a big crime, or at least a decent crime, every day people need a good crime so they'll have something to talk about at the dinner table. You don't know what my phone's been like. Journalists call here every day, every single day, those bastards call here, you say, well, a woman died in bed at her home, she was sleeping alongside her two small children and a stray bullet caught her in the heart. Is that all? they say. Stray bullets don't count. You know, they say, the victim, fuck the victim. We want to clobber someone. You know how it is, they say, the lions are hungry. And the lions are them. Us, I mean. Everybody, in general. So let's hope some crazy comes along right away. But I don't want to discourage you. In fact, things are going well. You just have to go on doing what you're doing, deny, deny, deny. And not open your mouth to say anything about anyone, because when you get out of here, chum, you're going to need your friends. And need me more than the rest. Need your clients. And they, all of us, need to be in a good situation to help you. I have my own private weather forecaster here in my brain. And my forecaster says that the storm has passed. As a matter of fact, yesterday, watching television, I saw for the first time a newscast that didn't mention you, or the kid. I didn't see any bishops demanding anything, that's a sign things are getting better. It means we're almost home. Stay calm, you're going to get out of this in a little while. You'll see.

A photo of Santana, smiling. A statement: I didn't do anything exceptional, I just carried out the law. It was about my arrest. Other newspapers also. Santana always smiling, always saying he'd only done his duty.

I'll bet, Enoque said, I'll bet Santana didn't give you these newspapers to read. You don't understand, I said, it's to throw them off the track, we agreed on it, it's all a set-up. No way, Enoque said, Santana is selling you out. He did two things with your arrest; he got the cops off his back, that is, he thinks he did. There's not a day somebody doesn't go by Alpha asking questions about him. They're going to get Santana, you can bet on it. What's the second? I asked. Second what? Enoque replied. You said Santana did two things with my arrest. I want to know what the second thing is. The second thing? he answered. The second thing is this circus here, showing up in the papers every day, that's the second thing he did. He enjoys it, the faggot. You never saw the comb he carries around in his pocket? All he has to do is see a mirror and he takes out the comb and combs his hair, totally shameless, does it in front of anybody, a faggot, a perfect faggot. Santana's going to find a way of getting me out of here, I said. Yeah, sure he is, Enoque said, Santana is a great guy, I remember how great he was with Marcão. That was different, I said. Different my ass. He's shit scared you'll open your mouth. He's stringing you along. That's all, I just wanted to open your eyes. Take this, he said. A penknife. It was Marcão's, that penknife, he said. Robinson gave it to him.

I didn't let it worry me. Not a bit. If Santana had weapons to fuck me, I had weapons of my own to fuck with him. Why would he be getting ready to fuck me? My arrest had been a gentlemen's agreement. It was a farce. All I needed was to have a little patience, that was all. And sleep with the knife under my pillow.

There was this really cool black guy in my cell. I enjoyed talking with him. He taught me to play checkers, we used to play checkers all day long, he was real good at it. He said he knew how to play chess, but when the chessboard arrived, arranged through one of my dozen lawyers, I saw it wasn't true, he didn't know how to play chess. Playing checkers is the first step, he said. You don't even know how to play checkers right and you want to play chess? A phoney, that guy, but I liked him.

So, the fact is that two days after Enoque came to see me, I was with Érica in my dreams, we were going to the movies, we were about to leave, getting into my car, when I woke with a pillow covering my face, somebody trying to suffocate me. I thought I was going to die, I was already dizzy, a buzzing in my head, my hand bumped into something cold, a blade, the penknife that Enoque had given me. I grabbed it and stabbed, I don't know where I stabbed, the pillow loosened, I managed to breathe in some air, I got out of bed, still dizzy, I just wanted to breathe, and it was only after getting my lungs back in order that I saw my black friend on the floor, the knife in his belly. You killed me, he said. He was speaking very softly, and, I don't know why, I started speaking very softly too. I put him on the bed, took out the knife, it hadn't gone very far in, I said, you'll be fine. I took my T-shirt, wetted it in water and started cleaning the wound. Always speaking very softly, so softly that none of the other cellmates woke up. You can tell me, he said, you can tell me I'm going to die, it's better to say so right off, if I'm going to die, he said, if I'm going to die I'd rather know the truth, you must have gotten me in the heart, did you get my heart? No, I answered. What about my lungs, you can tell me, did you get my lungs? It was nothing, I said, I was whispering, and it hadn't been anything, it was just a jab, I mean, it must have been just a jab, at least that's what it looked like. It was Santana, he said. It was Santana who ordered me to kill you.

It hit me there, right in the liver, a bitter taste came into my mouth and an electric current ran through my veins, my hands burned, the knife burned, I stabbed, my brain too, burned, I stabbed the knife in his belly over thirty times, stabbed, until the tenth stab he was wide awake, I stuck it

203

in, he didn't even let out a moan, the son of a bitch, he just watched me stab him, then he fainted, the black guy, and then he died, and then I stabbed him a lot more times just to make sure he was dead.

I cleaned my knife, put everything away, climbed onto my bunk and waited for daybreak.

Santana, that faggot. He would get his soon enough.

Somebody said this before: believing in mankind is a type of suicide.

38

When anyone dies in a cell, nobody knows anything. I just know I woke up and the guy was dead, that's what you say, and even if you do know something you're not crazy enough to say anything. Santana was at a loss, he didn't know if the black guy had tried to kill me, didn't know who'd killed the black guy, he was really at a loss. He called me all the time, this isn't an interrogation, he said, but you're the only person who can clear this up for me. Today it was that black man, he said. Tomorrow it could be you. Just look at what I had to listen to. Those guys are really good, I said, they kill without letting out a sound, those guys would be good working at Alpha, I said. He smelled a rat, of course, but I had decided not to give Santana a single thing more, I was like an actor, master of the situation. I'm worried, Santana said, could they have been trying to kill you? he asked.

Scum of the earth know no limits. They go on and on, to infinity if you let them. Who would want to kill me? I asked. You never know, Santana said, the guys here are so anxious to get you, wouldn't it be better if I try to have you transferred right away to another prison? he said, the scum. Listen, Santana, I'm not leaving here. And if I leave here, it'll be a violation of our understanding, I said.

He was going to get me transferred. Or send another guy to kill me. There wasn't any time, I had to act fast.

Fifteen thousand dollars is the price you have to pay. People think it's hard to escape from prison. What's hard is staying in prison. Escaping is easy. You just have to put everything up front, the fifteen thousand. After I decided to escape, no one did anything to stop me.

Follow the instructions: you buy the policemen on watch. You wait till Sunday night. You overpower the cops at the precinct, using the gun that Enoque brought you. Overpower is a figure of speech, the guys were already paid off, it's all for show. It's also part of the show that you shoot one of them in the leg, so the drama will look more realistic. You go to the weapons area, where the police arsenal is kept, if you're really enraged you kill the guy in charge of the arsenal; you can also let the guy live, that depends on your mood, but it's a good idea to handcuff him. I killed him. You take three machine guns, three revolvers, ammunition, cuffs, you leave the cops bound and gagged. And you walk out the front door. The whole thing takes five minutes. I did something else as well, I stuck a note in the mouth of one of them: Santana, I'll only come back here dead.

Enoque was waiting for me outside, with a car.

It wasn't hard at all. I set everything up in two days.

Enoque had sold my machine guns and the rest of the money he got through my twelve lawyers, the fifteen thousand. I have the impression I didn't ask for enough from those bastards. If I'd asked for a limousine they'd probably have given it to me; of course, a limousine, let's get a limousine for our friend.

Enoque and I stayed at a hotel downtown.

Didn't I tell you, Érica said in the dream, didn't I tell you those guys were lowlifes? How long are we going to stay in this flea-trap? We have to get out of town right away, she said. Let's go to Roraima. We can buy a ranch there. Roraima, Amapá, Macapá, that's not even really Brazil, they're not going to look for you there, outside Brazil.

It was a long night. I would wake up and fall asleep again, wake and sleep, the bed in the hotel was terrible. Each time I woke, the dream would seem to go on, the dream came outside, came into the hotel room, that's what seemed to be happening, except that Érica didn't come with it, she stayed behind, locked inside me. And when I returned to myself, there inside, she wasn't always there. Sometimes she was in the room, someone inside me told me that, she went to look for you in the bedroom, then I'd open my eyes to see if she was in the room. I wasn't the same guy anymore. I had changed. They had changed me. I wanted to talk about that with Érica, in the dream, but I kept forgetting. When I did remember, she'd left the dream. Or else, just as I was about to tell her, I'd wake up. I wanted so much to find out about Érica, I wanted so much to tell her, Érica, I understand everything you tried to say. Érica, I understand why you ran away from me. I wanted to tell Érica that ever since that black guy tried to kill me, something was born inside my liver, I felt it. A kind of cancer. A kind of light, something that illuminated my liver. I lost my juice that day, the juice in our blood that dissolves all the rotten things we're forced to swallow. A powerful hate was born in my heart, and I can say this, that hatred came to be the part of me that I liked most. It was also the only thing I wanted to keep, the only thing I was afraid of losing, my hate. I couldn't go near Alpha, my apartment, police swarming all over the place. I had lost everything. But I didn't care about any of that, there comes a time when the only thing that doesn't matter is money. Money is shit. I didn't care, I loved hate, and I didn't want to lose it. I fed it every day, in the best way possible. Except for my hate, I was a repugnant being just like those guys I hated. Dr Carvalho, a son of a bitch, and even so he threw me out of his house, shouting, mangy dog, he screamed. He was at the top of my list. No, Santana was at the top of the list. I couldn't stop anymore. Suddenly, I understood everything, that business about over here and over there, I've already mentioned that, but it was the black guy who hit me over the head with the truth. I was the revolver for those guys. Peace. They need a revolver because everybody wants to steal their laserdisk player. Their Miami. Rape their daughters. Their fear. Their security. They have no peace, they're all the time saying that, we have no peace. I was the killer, that was it. Peace. Now that the shit had begun to stink, they wanted to chuck the revolver into the river, they wanted to get rid of the proof. Discard after use, like you see on packaging.

I spent all night thinking about these things, I was late getting out of bed. When I got up, Enoque had already bought the newspapers. You talk in your sleep, he said.

I took a look at the crime pages. The effect had been good. My escape had brought down the jail superintendent. And all the cops on that watch. And there were still other guys to bring down too. The first of them would be that night.

★   ★   ★

I parked the car at the corner and waited. There was a vehicle in front of Santana's house. He must be afraid, the faggot, Enoque said. We turned on the radio, on one of the stations there was a report about my escape. It was an inside job, they said, he had the help of the police. They suspected Santana, who had already been called to testify before Internal Affairs. The announcer: the Secretary for Safety has established a board of inquiry to investigate the escape and promises to punish those responsible. The secretary also said that the Escaped Fugitives Department of the State Criminal Investigation Division is fully deployed to search for the South Zone Killer, and that the governor is personally following the investigations. The South Zone Killer. That's what they were calling me now. Those guys love to raise a stink, Enoque said. We've killed a lot of street kids just like that skateboarder, a lot, I myself, I don't know, I've killed over thirty, nobody cared. Now just because the kid's father is a pediatrician, those guys are funny, don't you think?

A quarter to ten, the right time. I think, I said, I think you should call the hotel and tell Érica we're going to be late. Enoque looked at me wide-eyed. He laughed. You said it so seriously, he said, that I almost thought it was the truth. I laughed too. I wanted her to be there, I said. It was what I wanted more than anything in the world, Érica. Any news of her? Enoque asked. No, I said. I liked her, Érica, Enoque said. A real great girl, Érica. Once she told me, Enoque, one of these days I'm going to do something. I'm going to buy a truck and drive all over. Maybe that's what she did, became a truck driver, said Enoque. You think, Máiquel, she could have become a truck driver?

Four policemen came out of Santana's house, got into the parked vehicle, and left. He'll be coming out soon, I said. I don't know, Enoque said, I kind of doubt he'll go there tonight. I was certain Santana was going to the barbecue restaurant, Tuesday was the day for the barbecue restaurant, and people hate to change their habits, and it was more than a habit; if Santana didn't eat his weekly cow, he'd die.

Right on the money. Santana and his family got into the car. Straight to the barbecue restaurant. They got out, the two sons spitting images of their father, with bellies just like their father, beef eaters. His wife, unbelievable how sickening that woman was to me. All flaccid, frosted hair, women like her just love frosted hair. I frosted my hair, she always used to tell Érica, every time we got together, frosted it, frosted it. A cow, that's what she was. Now? Enoque asked. A little longer, I said. I wanted to wait till the meat arrived at the table.

Santana had his snout buried in a pool of blood, the dish. He was eating, if you can call that eating. He swallowed the chunks of meat without chewing, the pig. He must have had a piranha in his stomach, feeding that piranha inside him wasn't easy. He didn't see me approaching. The one who saw me was the frosted woman. She turned pale, nudged her husband. Take the children outside, I said.

How's the meat? I asked. Good, he said. Sit down, let's talk. Talk, I said, you want to talk? These types are really impressive, they use you, they try to throw you away, they try to kill you, and if anything goes wrong they say, let's talk. Talk about what? About that black guy? Listen, Máiquel, wait, we're going to get a few things straight, he said. I shot. I shot him in the face, you can't imagine what that's like, a 9mm Beretta pistol, right in the lowlife's face.

Later I found out they had to seal Santana's coffin. They couldn't find all the pieces of his brain that were scattered around the restaurant.

39

Look what I brought you, I said, showing her a small envelope. Gabriela leaped from the bed, excited, my God, how wonderful, finally. I thought you really didn't like me, she said. You can't imagine, this is the first weekend I've been out of the clinic, I'm dry.

Gabriela spread two lines, snorted. Then her body jerked, wow, she said, pure. It's magic, she said. Just look, two minutes ago I was like an empty sack, collapsed there on the bed, now, you know, that feeling of greatness, shit, I can even think about going out somewhere, let's go somewhere, how'd you get in the house? Through the door, I said, it was open.

Will you take me somewhere? Except we'll have to go out the window. You can't imagine how my father, the asshole, is keeping tabs on me. No, I said, we can't go somewhere.

She looked at me. Cunning. She ran her tongue over her lips. She went to the door, locked it. She came back, sat down beside me. Very close, her legs exposed. They were nothing to turn up your nose at. Gabriela took my hand, put it on her pussy, do you have any more coke? she said. Do you want to fuck? I asked.

Gabriela took my hand away. She was embarrassed, that is, she pretended she was embarrassed, and that turned me on even more. Speak up, Gabriela, do you want to fuck me? I've got lots of coke to give you.

She didn't answer, she gave a dirty little laugh. You can say it, Gabriela, what's the problem? People fuck. Your father fucks, your mother fucks, your mother fucks your father's friends, your father fucks his patients, what's the problem?

Gabriela became disoriented. Her little let's-fuck game was out of control.

Say it, Gabriela: I want to fuck.

Nothing, Gabriela didn't obey me. I contained my irritation.

Hey, Gabriela, I thought you were more with it than that. What's the problem, is it the word fuck? OK. Let's change it. Copulate, do you prefer copulate? Copulate sounds like something a horse does, don't you think? How about screw? Screw is good. Come on, say it, I want to hear it from your mouth. Gabriela looked at the floor. I know, you prefer get it on. Let's get it on. You know what I think of the phrase get it on? Queers use it. Half-fucking. Shit fucking. You know, those guys who don't enjoy fucking, they say get it on, they climb on top of you, empty their come on you and leave, I don't call that fucking, do you, Gabriela?

Gabriela was somber.

Come on, Gabriela, come on, I want to hear it from your mouth. Fuck me. Fuck me, say it, Máiquel, fuck me with your enormous prick. Think of the coke, Gabriela.

She said it very softly but I heard her, fuck me. What? I asked, what did you say? You want me to fuck you? Yeah, she said. Then say it, I ordered. I want it, she said. The entire phrase, I said: I want you to fuck me. I want you to fuck me, she repeated. Ah, that's more like it, take off your clothes, I said, and get on the bed. She obeyed. She was totally naked on the bed. Gabriela was foxy, she might be a good lay. Spread your legs, I said. She spread them.

The problem, Gabriela, I said, the problem is that today I don't feel like fucking. I turned my back and left.

Gabriela stayed there, her legs spread. To think that I killed a guy because of that cow.

Dr Carvalho leaped out of bed as soon as he saw me, tried to reach the telephone. I was quicker, I yanked the cord out of the wall. His wife was in the shower, I could hear the noise. Máiquel, he said, keep calm. Be careful. Careful is for people who cross the street, I said, I'm not crossing the street. Dr Carvalho limped back and forth, his nice white dressing robe. Take off the robe, I said, pointing the gun. I don't want to get your nice white robe dirty, it doesn't deserve it, the robe. It was a pleasure to see Dr Carvalho, naked, limping, pot-bellied, shit scared, a pleasure to see. I aimed and hit him right in the middle of that belly full of shit.

40

The car was stolen, Enoque's work. We were heading for the south. No destination. We traveled all night. When the sun was rising we stopped in a small town that we came across. We ate at a bar, Enoque found the bar owner strange, could he have recognized us? No, I said. Country people are like that. They've got that crappy look on their faces.

We drove a bit more, found an abandoned construction site, the town's asylum. It was written there, São Francisco Asylum. We hid the car. You're crazy, Enoque said when he saw me take the vodka bottle out of the trunk, what are you going to do with that? We can't drink, he said. We can't sleep.

I opened the bottle of vodka, I wanted to be quiet, thinking about Érica, remembering the two of us, her teaching me to dance, right after Cledir died. OK, Érica said, I'll teach you to dance, but you'll have to loosen up, you're too stiff. Come on, do it like this, relax your shoulders, rock, she said, this isn't slow-dance music, it's not two up, two back, it's

214

whatever you want it to be, but it's not a samba either, pull in that hip, for God's sake, you know I hate the samba, Érica said. I didn't want to dance, I pushed against Érica, ever so slowly, she fell onto the bed. I fell on top of her, kisses. You know, Máiquel, sometimes I think about whether it'll always be like this, this love, this desire to fuck, will it always be this way, or will you get tired of me?

Enoque wouldn't let me think, he wanted to talk. He was afraid. You think they're going to catch us? he asked me.

Sometimes, I said, sometimes I have the impression that the world has turned its back on man, man his back on God, God his back on the world, a total mess, don't you agree?

Enoque didn't know how to carry on a conversation. I had to talk to myself. A total mess, it might be that, I said, or it might be other things too. And I didn't say anything else to Enoque. I didn't even know why I was saying all that. I wasn't interested in that, in others. They could fuck themselves. The whole world could fuck itself too. What I wanted was to drink vodka, think about Érica, and make it to Argentina as fast as possible.

If Érica had been with me, she'd have said: You went wrong because you stayed there and made it easy for those guys.

Érica, I wanted so badly to tell you this. So badly. Kamikaze, remember? I have a theory, Érica. Man, Érica, man when he licks at fame loses his character. That's what it is. You get famous and the problem of fame is that it makes you believe what others say about you. You enter that landscape, it's blue, and you start slipping in that blue mud, you go rolling down the hill until you're completely fucked up. That's what happened to me. I can't say it took me a long time to learn the lesson. I learned it too fast, I learned it the very first day, learned it every day, to tell the truth. But I would learn and do everything to forget it the next day, that was the problem. Success, Érica, success, it's a rule, success can't last. Success demands certain things, demands a fall, basically, a fall, the people who think you're a success, they demand you fall into the abyss. A slow fall, they want to go on amusing themselves, they demand that. They demand you do something freaky, demand that you drink, that you have drug problems. It's good too if you have problems with the police, because of the drug problem. They demand you frequently go in and out of clinics for crazies. Rehab clinics, they like that, not only because you're trying to crawl out of the shit, but because it gives them a chance to feel sorry for you. That's the best part of it for them, pity. You have to do all that, success demands such things. And you have to kill too. That's also part of success. In that sense, my career was perfect. I followed the manual to the letter. All that was left was to kill myself, but that never entered my mind.

The house is surrounded, there's no way out.

I got up, startled. Enoque wasn't there, he'd left to get cigarettes, a note on the floor, I'll be right back. This is Colonel Alfredo, you're surrounded and the best thing is to give yourself up. We have thirty men here. You can choose. You can come out with your hands up and no problem. Or, we're coming in. And we're coming in shooting. And there are thirty men, he said. I know you can hear me, I'll count to five.

One. I dragged myself to the door, I wanted to see the scene. Glorious. Lots of vehicles. Behind them, the men, all armed, in firing position. I couldn't see anything, I dragged myself to the other side, nothing, I couldn't see the men. Two. I got my machine gun, my revolver. I loaded. If they were thinking it would be easy, they were wrong. I wasn't desperate. Three. I thought about Érica, about Samantha. I kissed both of them. Four. I'm not going to die, love. Five.

I opened the door with the machine gun in my hand. It was strange. Them. There was no one there. Me. No one. Wind. I thought they'd concealed themselves, I got confused, no one appeared. You want to kill me? I shouted. Here I am, you sons of bitches. Come on, kill me. Nothing, only the sound of my boot, I was alone in that abandoned asylum. The voice, one, the men, two, wind, the guns, three, they weren't there, four, they were inside me, five, in my head. That wasn't good. They couldn't stay inside me. Inside me, I belonged to myself. And now those disgusting guys wanted to come in too, inside me. I wouldn't permit it. Never. Those guys would never come in again, I would close the doors tight, only Érica would stay inside there, Érica, yes. She could stay inside.

Enoque arrived, sounding the horn, I got into the car, let's blow this place, he said, I've got a bad feeling, I drove around the town, went to buy cigarettes, I don't know, there's something in the air. Enoque thought they'd already found us. They're on our trail, he said, I can feel it.

We got on the highway, with me at the wheel. A cold wind. Enoque turned on the radio. The police, the announcer said, still have not found the criminal known as Máiquel, accused of more than — I stuck my foot through the radio, smashed the piece of crap. I stopped the car. Get out, I told Enoque, they're not after you. I pushed him out of the car and tore off. I didn't want to know anything about what was happening, I wanted to leave everything behind, go on until I found a hole and buried myself in it, in the hole, hiding, in the hole, until the cold was gone, until it was time to come out.